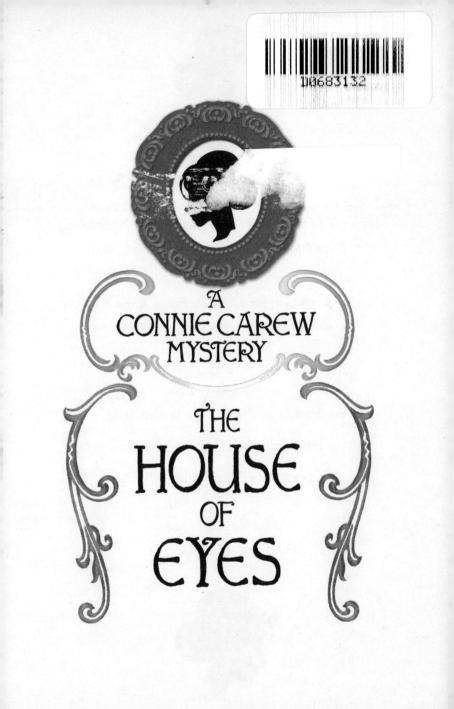

A
CONNIE CAREW
MYSTERY

THE

HOUSE

OF

EYES

Patricia Elliott

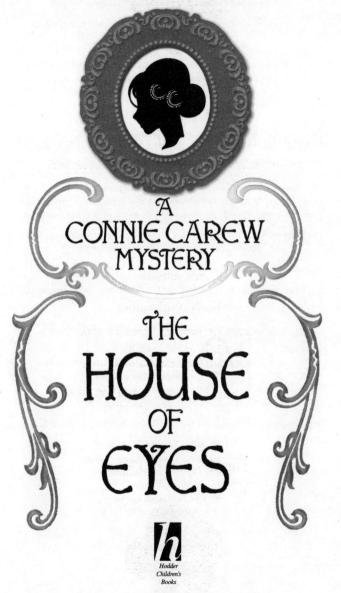

A
CONNIE CAREW
MYSTERY

THE
HOUSE
OF
EYES

Hodder
Children's
Books

a division of Hachette Children's Group

With thanks to my lawyer friend, Robin Peile, and to Emily Cartwright
and Laurence Akehurst of the London Transport Museum

First published in Great Britain in 2015 by Hodder Children's Books

A Catalogue record for this book is available from the British Library

Typeset in Baskerville by Avon DataSet Ltd, Bidford-on-Avon, Warwickshire

ISBN 978 1 444 92469 5

The paper and board used in the book are from wood from responsible sources.

Hodder Children's Books
An imprint of Hachette Children's Group
Part of Hodder & Stoughton
Carmelite House
50 Victoria Embankment
London EC4Y 0DZ

An Hachette UK Company
www.hachette.co.uk

For my brother Michael, who always
listened to my stories

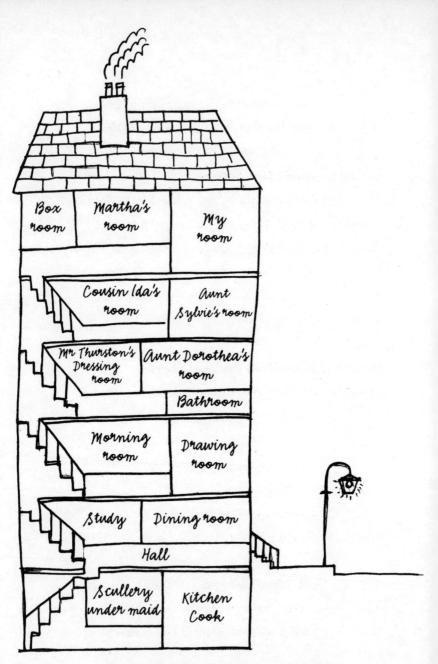

Plan of the house in Alfred Place West,
drawn by Miss Constance C. Carew

From an early notebook of Miss Constance Carew, Anthropologist, on first arrival at Alfred Place West, London, SW

Habitat: Second Floor Bedroom

Name: Dorothea Thurston (Mrs), aunt to C. Carew

Appearance: tall, thin, sad face

Habits: does not like going out (because of a Tragedy in her past) does not talk very much (because of the above) does not like giving hugs

Nature: a Gloomy (but Special) Person

Habitat: Second Floor Dressing-Room

Name: Harold Thurston, step-uncle to C. Carew married to Dorothea Thurston above

Appearance: slug-like, huge

Habits: puts Macassar oil on hair
wears creaky corset
bosses Aunt Dorothea

Nature: an Angry Person

Habitat: Third Floor Bedroom

Name: Sylvie Fairbanks (spinster), aunt to C. Carew older sister of Dorothea Thurston above

1

Appearance: wears funny clothes. Has no hair
Habits: talks a lot, mostly to herself
          sees Things that aren't there
Nature: a Happy Person on the whole
          also a Clever Person (though only C.C. knows
          this)

Habitat: Fourth Floor Attic Room (next to C. Carew)
Name: Martha – not sure of surname
          maid to household
Appearance: V. clean and neat
Habits: snores at night
Nature: a Cheerful, Kind & Nice Person

On a bright but chilly afternoon in early May 1909, a young girl of about twelve was chivvying two middle-aged ladies along a street in London's South Kensington. Her name was Constance Clementine Carew and she was on her way to a séance to raise her cousin Ida from the dead.

Not that Connie believed in that sort of thing. She considered herself a scientist, made for this great age of scientific discovery. She had already decided she would be an anthropologist when she was older and travel the world to study its peoples.

It had been Aunt Sylvie's idea to go to the séance. When Connie had taken in her tea tray the day before her aunt had held out a card, her short-sighted eyes gleaming. 'Read this, dear! It popped through the letterbox right at my feet, just as if it was meant for us!'

Connie took it, mystified.

Communicate With Your Loved Ones!
Madame Emerald Vichani. Renowned Medium
and Necromancer
Recommended by the Brompton
Spiritualist Society
Private sittings arranged for the Aristocracy
and Gentry
Séances at 30 Pelham Crescent every Wednesday

(and in very small letters at the bottom)

Fee payable on entry

'The truth will out, you know,' said Aunt Sylvie.

'What truth?' Connie said crossly, as she handed the card back. She was used to her aunt's fey ways but sometimes they irritated her. Aunt Sylvie believed that she could see things others could not, no matter how often Connie pointed out that 'they' were not there in the first place.

'Why, what happened to little Ida,' said her aunt. 'Only think, we might get a message from the other side! Now that would cheer dear Dorothea no end, put a stop to her glooms.'

'But Aunt Sylvie, you know it's all nonsense! The dead can't speak to us!'

4

'Oh, no, my dear, you are quite mistaken.' Her aunt looked as excited as a child. 'Why Mr Conan Doyle himself believes they can. He attends séances, so I have heard. And so did our dear late Queen!' She tapped the card. 'We shall go tomorrow, the three of us.'

Connie shook her head. 'Poots is taking me to the British Museum.'

Aunt Sylvie sagged in her chair. 'But I cannot manage Dorothea without you! Besides, did you not visit the museum only last week?'

'But one day I mean to be the most famous anthropologist in the world, Aunt Sylvie!'

Her aunt pressed her lips together. 'Women should not have professions.'

'But this is a new age!' Connie whirled round the room and flung out her arms. 'A new king, a new century! Things have changed!'

'And I'm adrift in it all, child.' Aunt Sylvie sighed. 'Meanwhile, this may be a chance to get my sister out of the house at last. It would be a start, at least.' She looked up at Connie plaintively. 'You will help me take her, won't you, dear?'

So in the end Connie had reluctantly agreed to go. She could not let her aunts wander off alone into the

5

wilderness of London's streets and, after all, a séance might be a fascinating opportunity for scientific research. Perhaps she should not pass it up.

Aunt Dorothea had not stepped outside the house in Alfred Place West for some years. Connie and Aunt Sylvie had had to hold on to her firmly, for she looked so dazed by the hurrying people, the rumble and rush of carriages, the clatter of horses' hooves, that it seemed she might faint on the pavement in a slither of her old-fashioned mourning skirts.

Progress was slow as they made their way through the sunlit streets, but Aunt Sylvie said it was not worth hiring a hansom cab to go so short a distance and anyway the only money they had between them, after a thorough search of Aunt Sylvie's cluttered bedroom, amounted to no more than a rather dusty guinea coin found under the mahogany wardrobe and which must be saved to pay for the séance.

People turned their heads to stare at them curiously: the tall woman with frightened eyes, stiff and pale as a waxwork, being helped along by a rounder, shorter one, whose face was hidden beneath an enormous, somewhat battered hat, its several feathers thrusting dangerously in all directions. They were led by a girl in a straw boater set at a jaunty angle, who marched ahead with a decided step and straight back, and though she possessed no particular looks there was something about her that held the gaze of the passers-by.

Connie consulted the card, now rather dog-eared and crumpled. They had arrived at the right address. She took hold of the knocker and rapped firmly on the front door.

It was opened by a sour-faced young maid, who looked at them suspiciously under her frilled cap.

'We've come to attend the séance,' said Connie. 'Is Madame Vichani at home?'

The girl motioned them in silently and, as they stepped into the narrow hall, as if on cue a woman glided out of a door on the left. She was dressed in voluminous black velvet which contrasted with the rippling golden hair that cascaded down her back. It was about as convincing a wig as any of Aunt Sylvie's, for beneath the youthfully abundant hair her face was lined, though heavily rouged.

'Welcome,' she said softly. The guinea that Connie held out vanished magically into the folds of her skirt. 'We are always pleased to have newcomers at our sittings.' Her voice was genteel, any accent banished long ago. She stepped closer and took Aunt Dorothea by the hand. 'You have had a loss, I see.'

To Connie's surprise Aunt Dorothea did not pull away; it was as if she had suddenly awoken from a long trance. She looked into the woman's face gratefully and her own, tight and drawn as it had been, relaxed.

'We are like a little club here,' said Madame Vichani. 'You will find plenty of fellow mourners and feel quite at home, I do assure you.'

It was true that the panelled drawing-room she then ushered them into was very like their own back in Alfred Place, but much dimmer, as the thick curtains had been drawn tightly, shutting out the daylight and any noise outside and making the room almost dark, save for a single candle burning in the centre of a large round table set in the middle. Connie suspected it had been placed there to create the right atmosphere, since she had already spotted the electric light hidden by a fringed shade hanging over the table.

Several people were seated around the table already, talking in hushed voices to their neighbours, just as if they were in church. There was no one of Connie's age.

Madame Vichani got to work briskly, closing the door, covering her golden hair in a black net and seating the three of them.

8

Connie took off her boater with a sigh of relief – the straw was pinching her forehead – and hung it over the back of her chair. She had been placed between a spindly elderly gentleman whose first visit it was also and who had come, he confided to her, in the hope of reaching his late wife, dead of a seizure; and Aunt Dorothea, who had now become passive again, her back slumped against the chair back as if she were half asleep. Aunt Sylvie sat opposite, her hat and wig pushed back, her eyes shining with excitement in the candlelight.

Among the shadowy shapes of heavy furniture Connie could make out a tall cabinet in one corner. Full-length curtains on either side had been drawn back to show that it was empty apart from a simple, upright chair. She jumped up to take a closer look, but to her astonishment and annoyance found her shoulders taken in a surprisingly firm grip by Madame Vichani and pushed down again before she could protest.

'Oh, no – Miss Carew, is it not?' she hissed. 'Once you are seated you do not rise again until after the session is over.' She turned to the circle around the table and spoke in a louder voice. 'Now, if you would all hold hands, we shall begin as we always do, with a hymn.'

Connie reached for Aunt Dorothea's limp hand and gave it a little squeeze of reassurance. Her other hand was clutched by the bony fingers of the elderly gentleman.

Everyone except Connie broke uncertainly into 'Abide With Me'. It was surely the very gloomiest hymn in the whole canon and singing it would only depress poor Aunt Dorothea further. Madame Vichani, giving Connie a reproving look, led them in a strong contralto, and as they came to the end of the first verse, she leaned over Connie in a waft of violet water and blew out the single candle.

They were immediately plunged into complete darkness. The voices stuttered to a halt.

Connie felt Aunt Dorothea's fingers quiver in hers; on her other side her neighbour breathed wheezily in the sudden silence. She was not aware that Madame Vichani, invisible in her black dress, the light absorbing the velvet, had stepped away from behind her chair, and she jumped when from somewhere in the darkness the medium's voice spoke, sounding deeper and more commanding than before.

'Please do not let go of each other's hands. I am about to enter the cabinet. In a little while we shall see who is to receive a message tonight.'

There couldn't be anything supernatural about Madame Vichani seeing her way through the darkness – she must know the arrangement of the room by heart; and, indeed, after a pause her voice sounded again from the corner where the cabinet stood, but slightly muffled, as if she had drawn the curtains over its opening.

'Is any spirit out there willing to come to me?'

Connie thought she could hear her heart thumping in the heavy silence – ridiculous when she knew it was all nonsense. She tried to be her usual rational self. When you were dead you were just old bones and dust!

All the same *that* was not a pleasant thought and she shivered despite herself. It occurred to her that if by some tiny chance it wasn't nonsense after all, her own dead parents might decide to take the opportunity to send her a message. They had been away in Egypt examining artefacts much of her childhood and had been distant and uninterested in her when they had come home, which meant that she had always been able to do almost exactly as she liked – rather as she did now. It would be perfectly dreadful if, encouraged by today's séance, they started materialising at odd moments, telling her what she should and shouldn't do.

The silence seemed to take on a different nature, pulsating with people's expectation; and the darkness grew thicker, pressing against Connie's eyes like fur.

Then from the corner cabinet a voice said, 'Why do you call me?'

It was not Madame Vichani's voice: it was a man's, deep and gruff.

The back of Connie's neck prickled in shock.

Madame Vichani appeared to recognise the spirit, which she addressed as 'Captain'. 'Do you have any messages for those present today?'

The Captain did indeed have messages and, it seemed, for most of the circle around the table. He growled them out to Madame Vichani, his words muffled, and she passed them on. One woman was not to worry: her sister was safe in the 'Summerland'; another was told that 'Frederick' was watching over her; Connie's neighbour heard that his 'burden of sadness' would soon lighten, at which he gave a great sob into his chest and almost let go of her hand.

It wasn't fair that after dragging Aunt Dorothea to the séance, there was no message for her. What a waste of a guinea!

For now that Connie's initial fright was over she did not believe for a moment that the voice of

12

the 'Captain' was anything but trickery.

The voice in the cabinet muttered into silence.

'We have lost the Captain's spirit,' said Madame Vichani sorrowfully. 'I think we will finish—' She stopped. 'But wait!' Another pause, then, 'Who are you?' She sounded startled.

'Ida,' said a girl's voice. 'I am Ida.'

Aunt Dorothea's hand in Connie's gave a convulsive jerk. She sat abruptly upright and uttered a little moan as the curtains of the cabinet parted, revealing a faint glow within.

The glow grew stronger, more luminous, and the figure of a girl, veiled in draperies of light, floated out. She did not move towards the fearful watchers at the table, but remained where she was, appearing to hover just above the carpet.

'Mama,' she said, in a sweet, low croon that was almost a song. 'Mama, I have waited so long, but now I am coming home.'

Aunt Dorothea's hand wrenched away from Connie's and her chair fell back with a thud. Connie felt a brush of air as her aunt rose to her feet. Her voice trembled with incredulity and hope.

'Ida? Ida? Is that really you?'

2

For the last four years, home to Connie had been the tall, gloomy, Victorian house in Alfred Place West, where she lived with her two aunts, Dorothea and Sylvie, and Aunt Dorothea's second husband, Harold Thurston.

The house was decaying slowly around them. Mr Thurston was miserly with money and the stair carpets were rotting, the gas lighting dim because he was too mean to put in the new electricity, and damp patches darkened the walls of the rooms. When Connie first arrived, aged eight, she had imagined they made the shapes of bulbous heads, rather like Mr Thurston's own head – as if he were present everywhere, watching.

The head had watched Connie in her attic room. She was only allowed a candle, as a gas lamp was thought too dangerous, and the head moved in the pale, flickering light. *'You're not wanted here,'* it seemed to say. *'Aunt Dorothea only took you in because she had to. That's why you're stuck up here in the attic.'*

The head watched Connie come in and go out and the head watched her write up her research notes in her special lined exercise book. After she had written them she used to stick out her tongue at the patch on the wall, but nothing had made Mr Thurston's head go away until she heard the thumping footsteps of Martha the maid, coming to bed next door.

Now that Connie was twelve and possessed of an appropriately rational mind for an anthropologist-in-training, she knew it was merely that the plaster hadn't dried out properly behind the wallpaper. It was still true, however, that Mr Thurston ruled over the household. And he had forbidden anyone to mention Ida's name.

'Why?' Connie had asked innocently, when she first arrived to live at Alfred Place West. She was having breakfast with Mr Thurston at the time, since her aunts took theirs in their bedrooms.

Mr Thurston did not look pleased at the prospect of having to share his quiet breakfasts in future with a small, inquisitive girl. His black brows snapped together and he shook out the ironed folds of his newspaper irritably. Under his clothes he wore a whalebone stomacher that creaked when he moved. It creaked now.

'It should be perfectly plain to you, Constance. Any mention of Ida only upsets your Aunt Dorothea. You can see how frail she is.'

'But surely we shouldn't forget Ida altogether?' Connie had said. 'One day she might come back.'

Indeed she hoped she would; she longed to have someone to play with.

'Ida is never coming back,' Mr Thurston said. 'Don't you understand? She was only two when she disappeared! She wouldn't remember anything of her previous life.'

'Did you offer a reward?' enquired Connie, with interest. Recently she had seen a bill pasted up on a wall in South Kensington offering five pounds for a lady's lost Pekinese. How much would a lost child be worth?

'A reward? Certainly not!' snapped Mr Thurston. 'I didn't want any old riff-raff turning up at the house! It was bad enough being pestered by the newspapers!'

To Connie, the story of her little lost cousin, Aunt Dorothea's daughter by her first husband, was delightfully mysterious. At that time she knew nothing of Mr Thurston's tempers, so she persisted.

'But she might be living somewhere near here! Shouldn't we look for her?'

Mr Thurston set down his coffee cup so sharply that it spilled; a brown stain spread across the tablecloth to Connie, who mopped at it helpfully with her napkin.

'We *have* looked for her,' Mr Thurston said so loudly and furiously that Connie looked up, startled. His face had gone very red and only the parting drawing a straight line through his oiled black hair remained white. 'The police looked for her. The detectives looked for her. *I* looked for her. Years ago. To no avail. She is dead. DEAD.'

Connie, wisely, had said nothing more.

As time went by, she learned that Ida, if she were still alive now, would have inherited a great deal of money from her late father on her eighteenth birthday. 'The Fairbanks Fortune', the newspapers had called it, according to Martha the maid, who had heard about it from Cook.

Connie wasn't interested in the Fairbanks fortune, but her longing for a cousin who would be a very special friend had never gone away. And now it was possible that Ida wasn't dead, after all. It was altogether an extremely interesting situation.

Neither Connie nor her aunts mentioned anything about the séance to Mr Thurston, of course, nor did they say anything to the servants. Both aunts were much too frightened of Mr Thurston's reaction if he heard about it, while Connie herself loved secrets.

There was only one person to whom she ever confided and that was Arthur, her young music tutor, who came to Alfred Place twice a week, for singing on Tuesdays and piano on Fridays. Since Connie had no ear for music they spent the time in happy conversation.

She told Arthur she wasn't exactly sure what she had seen at the séance. Aunt Sylvie was sitting up half the night to watch for a ghostly girl to float in through her bedroom door. But to Connie that girl had seemed very much alive, despite her strangely luminous frock.

'But it was jolly odd, Arthur. She wasn't there at the beginning and then she suddenly appeared!'

Arthur played a scale and pondered. He had long thin fingers, and the rest of him was long and thin as well. Being a student at the Royal College of Music, he rarely had enough money to buy new clothes, and his jackets and trousers looked shrunken. His ankles and wrists protruded, knobbly but elegant.

'The cabinet must have had a door at the back,' he said at last, having given it due thought. 'She must have been hiding behind it with the Captain.'

'There wasn't any room, Arthur! And what about the light? And she floated!'

'They can create extraordinary effects with electrical lights. Think of the theatre!'

Connie, who had never been to the theatre in her life, nodded doubtfully.

As for Aunt Dorothea, in the week after the séance she seemed to come out of the spell that had held her fast for so long. Connie would find her pacing up and down the hall while Mr Thurston was out at his club, or watching hopefully from the upper windows of the house.

Connie knew she was waiting for Ida's return, and she worried.

Otherwise life went on as usual in Alfred Place West. Martha dusted and cleaned; Cook interviewed girls for the new under-maid's position, something her mistress had always left to her; and Connie had her daily lessons with her governess, Miss Poots, in the stuffy upstairs morning-room that always smelled of Mr Thurston's macassar hair oil and the stale toast crusts Connie had stuffed behind the large mahogany sideboard.

'Couldn't we go to the British Museum this

afternoon, Pootsie?' said Connie, winding her arms around the governess's neck. Arthur wasn't coming until Friday and she was bored, so bored.

'Let me consult our timetable,' said Miss Poots primly, drawing a dog-eared diagram from her recticule. Connie's mother had insisted that her daughter have a proper education and her very last act on her final visit to England before contracting the cholera that killed her husband and herself in Egypt, was to engage Miss Poots, who had once studied at Oxford University.

Miss Poots frowned at the timetable and pursed her lips. 'No, this afternoon is definitely algebra, dear. And besides, look at the weather!'

It was true that outside the window the rain was pouring down and seemed set to last into the afternoon. But weather didn't bother Connie.

'We won't be wet inside the museum,' she pointed out. 'Besides, I don't believe algebra will be any use to an anthropologist.' She thought wistfully of the cases of skulls, spears and withered grass skirts waiting in vain for her eager inspection.

'Why don't you pop down to the kitchen and see if Cook has made us a cake for Elevenses?' said Miss Poots.

Connie knew her governess wanted to divert her. She wished she wouldn't treat her like a child; what with her aunts treating her like a grown-up most of the time, it was very confusing.

In the basement Aunt Dorothea was sitting at the kitchen table, giving instructions for the evening's dinner to Cook, so she slid over to where Martha was doing the ironing, thumping away with a flat-iron, hot from the range. The kitchen smelled of singed wool.

Martha winked at her and Connie was about to ask about the possibility of cake when a tentative knock sounded on the other side of the door that opened out into the area steps.

'I'll open it,' said Connie and skipped over the linoleum.

There was a girl, some years older than Connie, standing in the rain on the other side of the door. She was drenched, her much-patched coat wet through and drops falling from her shabby hat. She looked doubtfully at Connie in her starched white pinafore.

At the same moment Connie noticed a man loitering at the top of the area steps. He wore a flat cap pulled well down so that she couldn't see his face and was leaning on a stick.

'This is the right place, is it?' stammered the

girl. Her face was almost colourless; even her lips were pale.

'For what?' said Connie. The man had disappeared into the teeming rain.

'For the position.' The girl straightened up and wiped her wet face with a grubby glove. 'I've come about the position for an under-maid. I seen the ad in *The Lady*.'

'Then you'd better come in,' said Connie and the girl floated in behind her like a ghost.

Cook looked exasperated. 'I'm sorry for the interruption, madam,' she said to Connie's aunt. 'I've got nobody down for an interview this morning.' She turned to the girl accusingly. 'You're too early!'

She took a much scribbled-over sheet of paper from the table drawer and consulted her list of names, shaking her head.

'But you can't send her away,' protested Aunt Dorothea. 'Why, she's quite wet through!'

The girl gazed helplessly at Cook, then over at her would-be mistress. Her big blue eyes looked as if they would well over with tears at any moment.

'What's your name?' demanded Cook.

'Brown,' said the girl. 'Ida Brown.'

'Why, I've not even got you down!' said Cook,

looking at her paper. 'You're not from the agency, are you?'

'Did you say *Ida*?' breathed Aunt Dorothea.

3

Connie stared at the girl and so did Aunt Dorothea. Martha, sensing the sudden tension in the kitchen, stopped thumping with the iron and stared in turn. Even Cook looked up; she had been in the household as a young under-maid herself when Ida disappeared. But perhaps there had been too many false hopes raised over the years, for Connie saw her shake her head dismissively.

'Ida's not such an unusual name, madam. Where's your reference, girl?'

The girl had a stained leather bag clutched to her chest. Her face paler than ever, she snapped it open and fumbled inside, while rainwater from her dripping coat puddled at her feet.

'Sit down, Miss Brown,' said Aunt Dorothea gently, and pulled out a chair.

The girl started forward. The next moment she

gave a cry. 'Oh, me locket!' The chain had caught on the back of the chair.

'Wait,' Connie said, rushing forward. 'I'll undo the clasp. You'll break it otherwise.'

Cook sniffed. 'Jewellery shouldn't be worn to an interview, my girl.'

The chain was cheap, Connie could tell, the tarnished links crudely soldered together. But the locket itself, though delicate and tiny as a thumbnail, was finely wrought and looked as if it was made of real, gleaming gold.

Aunt Dorothea leaned forward in her chair. Her face was as pale as the girl's. 'Let me see, Connie.'

Connie dropped the locket and chain into her aunt's palm, while the girl watched, puzzled.

As if her aunt's fingers still kept a memory of doing so in the past, they found the hidden catch with ease and clicked it open.

Behind the glass of one half there was a baby-fine curl of palest gold; in the other half, a minuscule photograph of a young woman.

Connie's aunt nodded, her smile strange and crooked as if she wasn't sure whether to cry or laugh.

'I knew it was you, Ida! I knew it was you as soon as you came in. This is the christening locket you were wearing the day you went missing!'

Cook heaved a resigned sigh. 'Excuse me, madam, but it might be best not to leap to conclusions. It's all a bit sudden, if you don't mind me saying. We know nothing about this girl. She may be a common thief, out to bamboozle us all. May I have your permission to ask her a question?'

Aunt Dorothea nodded, her eyes brimming.

Cook turned to the girl and eyed her severely. 'Did you steal this locket?'

The girl drew herself up indignantly. 'No, I never did!'

'Where did you find this locket then?' demanded Cook.

'I've 'ad it all me life. It's mine, I swear it!'

Aunt Dorothea clasped her hands together. ' You're Ida, aren't you? Ida, my own dear child.'

'That's me name, all right,' said the girl.

'Be careful, madam,' said Cook. 'She could still be an imposter. And stop gawping, Martha!'

'I know my own flesh and blood,' said Aunt Dorothea stubbornly, standing up and putting her arms around the girl's wet shoulders.

Connie frowned; her aunt was not at all demonstrative usually. As the girl drew away in surprise, Aunt Dorothea touched a lock of her hair beneath the crumpled hat.

'Still the same colour! And she has kept my picture. Look, Cook! Can't you see the likeness between us?'

Cook examined the locket suspiciously and so did Connie, staring over her shoulder. The likeness was remarkable, Connie had to admit: the young woman in the photograph was an older version of the girl sitting at the table. There was the same frailty about them both, the same ethereal quality, and Aunt Dorothea's hair, before it had become streaked with grey with the shock of losing Ida, had once been the same pale gold as the girl's was now.

Tears began to stream down her aunt's face. 'Ida! My daughter!'

Cook had been convinced at last; her face softened.

'Well, blow me down with a feather!'

Of course her aunt wanted to ask the girl endless questions and Connie listened intently to all the answers, though she longed to ask some herself. Cook ordered Martha, whose mouth was still open, to make some tea and bring out the ginger cake, and bustled about, trying to hide her own tears.

Where had Ida been living all this time?

In an orphanage in West London, the Sisters of Hope. She had been helping with the little ones but now she was older she wanted to find a paid live-in position. She knew how old she was – nearly eighteen – because the locket had her name 'Ida' and birth date engraved on the back.

'That's right!' Aunt Dorothea cried, nodding at Cook.

Did she know when and how she had arrived at the orphanage?

She had been told that she had been found asleep on the doorstep in a banana crate, with the locket on a little gold chain around her baby neck and a dirty blanket to cover her. Under the blanket they had found a scrap of paper with 'Please take in this poor orphan' scrawled on it. She had been given the surname 'Brown' by the orphanage, she said.

'But your surname isn't Brown, it's Fairbanks, like my late dear husband's, and you aren't an orphan at all!' cried Aunt Dorothea, wiping her eyes with a lace hanky. 'You have a mother who grieved for you, who thought you were lost, or worse, dead! We all did. Me, your Aunt Sylvie and your stepfather.

You have relatives, Ida, and a cousin, Connie.'

'Constance Clementine Carew,' said Connie, 'How do you do?' and she thrust out her warm hand, which the girl took awkwardly in her cold, clammy one. She looked bewildered and rather frightened.

Aunt Dorothea clapped her hands. Usually she was a stiff, anxious woman who didn't show emotion, but now her pale cheeks were flushed and her eyes shone.

'We must take you upstairs and find you some dry clothes. Martha will draw you a hot bath. You can have your old room back again.'

'Lawks!' said Ida, her eyes wider than ever.

'Fancy, madam!' said Cook. 'It's like a miracle. If I hadn't put that advertisement in *The Lady* . . .'

'Won't the orphanage wonder where you are?' said Connie to Ida.

The girl shrugged her thin shoulders. 'They ain't going to bother their 'eads about one less mouth to feed, that's for sure.'

'Oh dear,' said Aunt Dorothea faintly. 'I think some elocution lessons may be needed, Ida dear.'

Ida looked even more alarmed. 'Wot's them?'

'What about the man who brought you here?' said Connie. 'Is he coming back for you?'

Ida's pale blue eyes fixed on her blankly. 'Wot man? I come 'ere on me own.'

Connie frowned.

She knew the girl was lying.

Connie quickly realised that everyone in the household wanted the girl to be long-lost Ida. Whether she was or not was another matter and Connie, as the only truly sensible person there, determined to take the responsibility of finding that out herself.

Of course, Aunt Sylvie was almost as overjoyed as Aunt Dorothea. She put the palm of her hand on Ida's forehead as if she were listening for something.

'Yes!' she exclaimed. 'You are indeed my niece, Ida! I feel the aura coming from you.' She took her hand away and whispered, 'We spoke to each other, didn't we?'

'I didn't say nothin',' said Ida, looking puzzled. She backed away, staring nervously at Aunt Sylvie, who was looking particularly mad that day, her wig awry and a counterpane trailing from her shoulders.

Aunt Sylvie smiled gently. 'Your *soul* spoke to me,

31

my dear. I know you have risen from the dead.'

'That's very rude,' said Ida, outraged. 'Are you sayin' I'm a corpse or summat?'

'Ida is very much alive, Aunt Sylvie,' said Connie.

'She needs feeding up, that's all,' said Aunt Dorothea.

'It's me natural look,' said Ida. 'You can't do nothing 'bout it. I won't say no to a decent supper, though.'

Ida looked around her old room with wonder, though she could hardly be remembering it from when she was two years old. The cot had been removed many years before, along with all the baby things, and there was now a bed and sensible grown-up furniture for visiting guests – not that many came to the house in Alfred Street West. Otherwise it was as dark and dingy as the other rooms. Luckily, Ida did not notice the faint but unmistakeable smell of damp; she was probably used to it in the orphanage.

Aunt Dorothea pulled a book from the bookcase. 'Do you remember this, Ida?' she said tremulously. '*Johnny Crow's Garden*? I used to show you the illustrations.'

'Why, I do remember them pictures!' said Ida.

She began to turn over the pages of woodcuts, while

Aunt Dorothea's anxious face lit with delight.

'What are we going to say to Mr Thurston – I mean Uncle Harold?' said Connie to her aunt.

He would not be pleased at having to share his breakfast time with *two* girls now. At last Connie would have someone to talk to, instead of a silence that was only broken by Mr Thurston's large yellow teeth crunching toast and Gentleman's Relish, and the occasional creak of his corset.

Aunt Dorothea said, surprisingly firmly for her, 'We shall tell your Uncle Harold that Ida has come back. That is all he needs to know. We shall say nothing about the séance or about how Ida arrived so miraculously today. You do understand, don't you, Connie?'

Connie did understand. She knew Mr Thurston would not approve. All the same she waited for his reaction to Ida's arrival with interest.

By the evening hour that Mr Thurston usually came home, Ida had been transformed. She wore a dark blue dinner dress belonging to Aunt Dorothea – for they were the same height – which set off her pale skin to perfection, and her hair was newly washed and put up.

She looked remarkably pretty but almost grown-up, thought Connie, dismayed.

They waited in the hall for Mr Thurston's arrival: Connie's two aunts and Connie herself and Martha, waiting to take Mr Thurston's coat. Aunt Dorothea warned Ida to keep out of sight on the first landing until she had told her husband the wonderful news.

Mr Thurston arrived in his usual abrupt way, banging open the front door and shaking out his umbrella so that drops spattered everywhere. He thrust his wet bowler hat and coat at Martha and stared at Aunt Dorothea in her dinner dress as if he could not believe his eyes.

'You're out of mourning! Why are you dressed like that? You never stay up to dinner! You're not well enough.'

'But I'm not tired at all today, Harold,' Aunt Dorothea said timidly, her courage appearing to seep away on seeing her husband. She clasped her hands together. 'Something has happened . . .' She paused while he frowned at her impatiently.

'What is it, Dorothea?'

'It's . . . it's that . . .' She struggled for words and then they burst out in a rush. 'Ida is found!'

Mr Thurston went as yellow as old cheese and clutched the umbrella-stand. 'What are you talking about? Who has found her?'

'She arrived here this morning, Harold, and she is truly my daughter – look, here she comes!'

Mr Thurston looked up and his expression altered. The usual high colour flooded back blotchily into his cheeks and he straightened himself with an effort. No one noticed this except Connie; all eyes were on the girl in the blue dress coming down the stairs, the two aunts standing close together, transfixed, and Martha, still clutching the wet coat and hat.

Ida put out her hand, her smile sweet. 'Pleased to meet you, sir.'

Mr Thurston took it and shook it – limply for him. 'Goodness me, this is tremendous news!' His tone was halting, as if he were trying to gather his wits. 'How did it happen?'

'It was quite by accident, sir,' said Ida eagerly. 'I sees the ad in *The Lady*, for an under-maid. And I had my locket wiv me, like I always do.'

'Your locket?'

She unfastened it from around the high neckline of her dress and gave it to him. He studied it, pursing his lips.

'I 'ad it as a baby, see. When I went missing,' she added helpfully.

35

'I believe I remember it.' He looked at her, frowning. 'We scoured London, you know, called in the police – detectives. My wife has been smitten with grief all these years. But here you are, and you have the locket to prove that you are Ida. Most convenient.'

'Yes, 'ere I am,' said Ida.

He handed the locket back to her. 'We shall just have to find another under-maid, won't we?' he said, in a joking way.

Connie was quite expecting Mr Thurston to ask Ida all sorts of questions, just as her aunt had done, but he did not.

'You don't mind, do you, Harold?' said Aunt Dorothea nervously. 'She must stay with us now, mustn't she, now that we have found her? She can't go back to her old life. She was living in an orphanage, poor child!'

'Perfectly dreadful,' breathed Aunt Sylvie, clutching her counterpane tighter. 'I sensed the unhappiness of the place emanating from her.'

'Of course she can stay here,' Mr Thurston said brusquely. 'She is a member of the family, after all. Now, if you'll excuse me, I shall go and dress for dinner.'

With that he brushed past the two anxious aunts

and, with scarcely a second glance at Ida, went up the stairs towards his dressing-room. Connie glimpsed his set face: it was inscrutable.

Mr Thurston had been uncharacteristically amenable to Ida staying. It was all very curious, especially as now Connie was no longer the only person in the household who suspected that Ida was not all that she seemed.

She had been watching Mr Thurston closely and knew that he didn't believe it either.

5

Since Connie had arrived in Alfred Place West she hadn't been invited to the houses of other families in the area. It was whispered that Mr Thurston had made his money 'in trade' and for some reason that Connie didn't understand, this made her an unsuitable friend for their children.

Once, and once only, she had been invited to the Cavendishes next door, to play with the twins.

Cecil and Claud were half her age and only wanted to be lifted on and off their rocking horse. In frustration, Connie, having lifted the chubby Cecil on for the fifth time, had pushed the horse a little too violently and it had rocked Cecil right over its head, in a nose-dive to the nursery floor, where he had screamed and screamed until Nanny came running.

Connie had never been asked again.

So all this time she had yearned for her own perfect,

special friend. And now she had Ida. What did it matter if she wasn't really her cousin at all?

She tried to wheedle out stories of the orphanage from Ida but Ida said, 'I'd rather not dwell on them times, Connie. It makes me sad to think of them now.'

'Was it so very dreadful?'

'Mrs Goodenough what runs it, she's a tartar, right enough. Mean and nasty. Glad to escape 'er.'

'Whereabouts is it?' Connie asked.

'Oh, down 'ammersmith way,' Ida said vaguely.

Connie invited Ida to visit her bedroom, where she had casually displayed a couple of her notebooks, carefully chosen, on the bed. Ida was impressed, but not in the way Connie hoped. 'Such neat writing!' she cried.

Aunt Dorothea whisked Ida up to Knightsbridge for new clothes and Connie, anxious not to miss a moment of her new companion and worried about her aunt's stamina or lack of it, tagged along to Harrods with them.

However, since the advent of Ida, Aunt Dorothea had undergone a miraculous recovery. It was as if she had been frozen in a long sleep and had woken up at last and begun to thaw. There was a sparkle in her eyes as she watched Ida parade up and down in a variety of costumes in front of the long mirrors. She had almost lost her anxious expression.

As she gave their address for delivery and signed the account for a large amount of money, Connie said, 'Won't Mr Thurston be cross?'

'Try to call him Uncle Harold, Connie. No, I've been lending him my money for years. It's high time I spent it how *I* wish for a change. Ida must be dressed properly.'

Connie felt a pang of jealousy which she quickly quashed. After all, she had never wanted for anything during the four years she had lived with her aunts.

'Now, Ida,' continued her aunt. 'You need new hats!'

'I gotta hat,' said Ida, patting it protectively.

'I'm afraid that hat of yours won't do at all. But before we go to the milliners in Old Bond Street, we'll go to Fuller's for tea.' Aunt Dorothea sighed happily. 'It's such a long time since I've been there!'

Connie cheered up at that. Fuller's did the most excellent cakes, with thin sugary icing and walnuts; once or twice Miss Poots had relented and taken her there after an educational outing to see London's historic sites.

They had a table in the window and it was while Aunt Dorothea was showing Ida the polite way to hold her teacup, that several young ladies who had been sitting at a table further in suddenly stood up and started shouting out, 'Votes for women! Give us the right too! Let women have their say!'

Ladies, discreetly sipping their Earl Grey tea after a satisfactory afternoon's shopping, gazed around in horror. Up in the gallery the band struck up a medley of light operetta music to drown out the agitation below.

But already the group had dispersed and were slipping from table to table, handing out leaflets before anyone could protest.

One landed on top of Connie's slice of cake and stuck to the icing.

She looked up. A girl of around Ida's age, with bright red hair tumbling down under her hat, winked at her. She wore a fashionable masculine shirt and tie and looked enviably dashing.

Then, just as suddenly, they had all gone, taking with them the red-haired girl.

Aunt Dorothea drew her lips together. 'Suffragettes! I've read about the damage they do to get noticed!'

'They didn't do any damage here,' said Connie.

She stared at the leaflet, which was printed on cheap paper with smudged ink. She had admired the style of the girl with red hair. But she wanted to be an anthropologist, not a suffragette. Unless she could be both, perhaps.

The tea room relaxed back into its usual soothing afternoon murmur. The band played the latest dance music softly in the background. Aunt Dorothea showed Ida the polite way to hold a knife. Connie finished her cake and looked out of the window.

There was a man loitering on the opposite pavement, leaning on his stick and staring at them under the peak of his flat cap. She was immediately sure that it was the same man she had seen at the top of the area steps when Ida first arrived.

'Look, Ida!' She tugged her arm, making her drop the knife. 'There's that man again! Don't you know him?'

'Wot man?' said Ida, looking round in bewilderment.

'Outside, not in here!' Connie said, in exasperation.

But he had disappeared round the corner. For someone with a stick he moved remarkably quickly.

Aunt Dorothea paid the bill and they stepped out into the pale, uncertain sunlight. It had been a most unpredictable summer so far and women didn't know whether to carry parasols or umbrellas. Connie's aunt snapped up her parasol now, which was why she almost fell over the man's stick as they rounded the corner.

'Oh goodness,' she said, flustered. 'I didn't see you! You poor man! I believe I trod on your foot.'

'No 'arm done, lady,' said the man, doffing his greasy cloth cap.

Beneath it his hair was thin and greying, the back of his head oddly flat. He stared at the three of them for a moment out of bold brown eyes and Connie stared back.

'Do I know you?' Aunt Dorothea said, in a puzzled way. 'You look familiar.'

'Plenty of us scrapin' a livin' where we can,' said the man, and the sudden bitterness in his voice made her step back. 'Years past, you've probably seen me tryin' to sleep in a gutter or on a doorstep with the rubbish, while you sweep past on your way to the opera or summat.'

'I'm sorry,' she said feebly and fumbled in her purse. 'Here's a shilling for you. Please take it.'

'I will and all,' said the man and he snatched at it and bit it. 'I expect you've plenty to spare.'

'Come along, girls,' said Aunt Dorothea, her voice trembling.

When Connie looked back the man had limped off

in the opposite direction. 'He was waiting for us,' she said. 'He'd been watching us and then he waited for us on purpose!'

'What a thing to happen in Regent's Street!' said her aunt, taking a deep breath. Connie knew how much she hated confrontations. 'In Oxford Street, perhaps, but not here! Such a seedy little man! The impudence of him!'

'Do you know him, Ida?' said Connie.

'Of course she doesn't, Connie!' However, her aunt suddenly looked unsure, as if she had remembered the sort of world Ida came from.

Ida shook her head indignantly. 'That beggar? Never seen 'im before in me life.'

But her face was white.

6

After an even more boring session at the milliners, where Aunt Dorothea encouraged Ida to try on endless different hats, they took a horse-drawn cab back to South Kensington. It happened that Mr Thurston arrived back at the same time, unusually early for him.

He banged the front door behind him and stared at Aunt Dorothea, who was giving her coat and parasol to Martha.

She jumped guiltily. 'Oh, we weren't expecting you till later, Harold. Have you had a good day?'

'I have not, as it happens, but that is beside the point. Why have you been out? You never go out!'

Aunt Dorothea gestured weakly at Connie and Ida, laden with shopping. 'We had to buy Ida some new clothes.' Connie noticed that she was stammering, as she always did when she talked to Mr Thurston.

'It must have tired you out. You know you're not strong enough.'

'Oh, but I feel so much better—' Aunt Dorothea began.

Mr Thurston interrupted her, his face very red. 'You're not well, Dorothea, you know that! If Ida needs new clothes she can buy them herself and put them on your Harrods account.'

'But, please, Harold . . .' Aunt Dorothea wrung her hands together. 'We had such fun, the girls and I! I'm sure the fresh air has done me good.'

Mr Thurston went on like a steam-roller, as if she hadn't spoken. Though Aunt Dorothea was tall, she was slight and he was as large and solid as a wardrobe.

'You mustn't leave the house again. It's too much for you, Dorothea. Now go and rest. I think you should have dinner in bed.'

'Well, perhaps I do feel a little fatigued,' said Aunt Dorothea meekly.

She looked diminished by Mr Thurston's outburst. She went slowly up the stairs, her head bent, like an old woman.

Mr Thurston seemed to want to keep her aunt a prisoner in her own house, as he always had done. Connie couldn't believe *that* was good for her health.

"'e's a bully, ain't 'e?' whispered Ida to Connie as they went up the stairs. 'I'm glad 'e's not my father!'

'Are you so very tired?' said Connie. 'Do you always do what Mr Thurston says?'

She looked anxiously at her aunt, who was sitting in bed, her face as white as a ghost though Martha had already lit the fire. Then she saw to her relief that it was only cold cream, which her aunt was tissuing off with the aid of a little mother-of-pearl-backed mirror. Mr Thurston had gone out for dinner at his club, so Connie, Ida and Aunt Sylvie had had the most enjoyable time together. It would have been even nicer if Aunt Dorothea had been with them.

Aunt Dorothea sighed. 'It's always easier to do what Uncle Harold says. He rescued me, you know.'

Connie knew the background to the story. Aunt Dorothea had been Connie's father's sister – like Aunt Sylvie, who had been the eldest of the three siblings. Aunt Dorothea had married an extremely rich man called Reginald Fairbanks and had been very happy; Aunt Sylvie had never married anyone but was happy in her own way.

But then Reg Fairbanks had died unexpectedly young of a heart attack, when Aunt Dorothea was pregnant with Ida, their first child.

'How exactly did Mr Thurston rescue you?' said Connie, frowning. It didn't seem to fit in at all with what she knew of Mr Thurston's character.

Her aunt sighed. 'I wasn't well after Ida's birth and I was still grieving for Reg. But then I met Harold and he − I don't know − took me over, organised everything.'

Was that a good reason to marry someone? Connie supposed it might be.

'And so you married him?'

'I wanted to show him how grateful I was,' said Aunt Dorothea defensively. She sat up straight against the pillows, as if she were justifying her decision. Her face had emerged beneath the cold cream, looking normal but harrassed.

She put down the mirror.

'I'll try to explain, Connie. Your Uncle Reg's will was very complicated, you see. He'd rewritten it when he knew I was having a baby. He had the Fairbanks inheritance to think about. He wanted the bulk of the money to go to our child on his or her eighteenth birthday. I think he thought he would always be around to provide for me. He never thought he would die so unexpectedly.'

'So you had nothing?'

'I had the money from Reg's life insurance and the very generous allowance he had always given me.' Aunt Dorothea flapped her hands. 'Oh, you're too young to understand, Connie! I shouldn't be talking to you like this.'

'But you always do,' Connie said gently.

'Of course, it occurred to me many times over the years that Ida might be dead . . .' Aunt Dorothea said, as if Connie hadn't spoken. She shivered and drew her eiderdown up closer. 'But now I need never think about that again.' She hesitated, then spoke more strongly. 'There's a cardboard box on the top shelf of the cupboard, Connie. Take it down and throw the contents on the fire. I don't need to keep them any more.'

The box was full of old newspaper cuttings, crisp and yellow. Connie read . . . **Little Lost Heiress** . . . **Empty Pram Mystery** . . . **No Ransom Asked** . . . before the fire had shrivelled them and spat them away up the chimney, as if it didn't like their taste.

Aunt Dorothea gave a great sigh and sat back against the pillows. 'Thank you.'

Connie came back to the bed. 'So you believe this

girl is really your Ida?' she said carefully.

'What do you mean?'

'It would be easy for her to pretend. She might be after the Fairbanks inheritance.'

'Connie! How can you say such a thing?'

'Well, she could have found that locket anywhere – in a pawnbroker's, or something.'

'Do you think I don't know my own child?'

'But she's not a child any more. Years have passed. She's a young woman now.'

'I can tell she's my daughter,' said her aunt flatly. 'But we'll have to go through the formalities. In order to inherit on her birthday she'll have to prove to the court that she really is Ida Fairbanks.'

'Does Ida know that?'

Aunt Dorothea sighed again, irritably this time. 'Not yet, but I'm sure she'll have no trouble convincing them. She's got the locket, after all.' She was wearing a hairnet to keep her hair out of the cold cream and now it made her expression look tight and drawn up too. 'Stop asking questions, Connie! You're making me feel even more tired.'

'You weren't feeling tired at all until Mr Thurston said you were,' Connie pointed out.

She bent to kiss her aunt goodnight, but her

aunt's slightly sticky cheek was as rigid as Martha's ironing-board.

Connie left the room. Her heart was heavy.

'You see, Arthur –' Connie said the following morning when she was thumping out her scales under his watchful eye '– actually I'm not sure I mind whether Ida's my cousin or not. But poor Aunt Dorothea will never recover if Ida turns out to be an imposter, out to steal the inheritance. What do you think I should do?'

There was a long pause while Arthur furrowed his brow wisely.

'Why don't you wait for the court's decision?' he said at last and then much more quickly, 'No, no, Connie! That should be middle C!'

'They'll all be stern men in white wigs,' said Connie, who knew nothing about court procedure, but had a vivid imagination. 'I don't think that locket will be enough proof. It will be awful for Aunt Dorothea. If I could find out more beforehand, then she'd be prepared . . .'

'And how will you do that?' said Arthur.

Connie wasn't sure. Yet.

After that it was time for her singing lesson.

She was growling out 'Pale Hands I Love' and Arthur had wandered over to the window where his back view was becoming increasingly agitated, when she heard a silvery voice humming the tune over her shoulder.

Connie turned round and so did Arthur.

It was Ida, looking very fetching, her pale gold ringlets, the result of curling tongs, cascading over one of her new morning dresses, a froth of pale blue which exactly matched her eyes.

Arthur's mouth dropped open and he goggled like a fish.

'You must be . . . ?'

'Miss Fairbanks,' said Ida, opening her eyes very wide. She glided over to Arthur in her long skirt and held out her hand, delicate but sadly chapped-looking still, despite slatherings of Elizabeth Arden's Orange Skin Food. 'You may call me Ida. Please to meet you, Mister . . . ?'

Arthur swallowed. 'Harker,' he said thickly and blushed.

'Well, then, Mister 'Arker, I'm to 'ave singin' lessons wiv you and Connie 'ere.'

At that moment Connie knew the days of confiding

in Arthur were over. He was clearly thrilled to have a pupil who had true musical potential – and was beautiful as well. Whether she was Ida Fairbanks or not mattered not a jot to him. His hands trembled as he turned the pages of the music book, struggling to explain the notes as Ida leaned over him, her smooth brow furrowed in concentration.

'Tomorrow we'll go to the British Museum,' Connie said later to Ida. 'It's Saturday, so no Pootsie!'

Ida clearly had no idea what thrills the British Museum had in store for her – if she had heard of the museum at all – but she had had an elocution lesson after singing. She moistened her lips.

'*Jolly good*,' she said carefully.

That evening Connie wrote up her notes on Ida in the last of the daylight, turning her back on her bedroom wall where the head was growing and becoming marked with darker, damper spots, like a measles rash.

Name: Ida Fairbanks (?)
(My long-lost cousin?)
Age: seventeen years (?)

*Habitat: formerly an orphanage (?) in Hammersmith, W London
now 4th floor, opposite Aunt Sylvie, Alfred Place W.
Appearance: V pale but definitely not ghost
Characteristics:*

Here Connie sucked the end of her pen and after some thought wrote:

*Likes new clothes / hats. Likes Fuller's walnut cake. Likes Arthur?
Right about Mr Thurston
Others to be confirmed on further acquaintance
Big Question: If Mr T. thinks Ida is imposter, why is he letting her stay here?*

She looked at what she had written and frowned. There were an awful lot of question marks.

'*It's up to you, Connie Carew!*' she muttered. If she didn't find the answers, no one else would.

7

She would start her investigation of Ida by springing questions on her when she was unprepared.

So the following morning, as she and Ida queued in the booking hall at South Kensington Underground station and Connie was searching in her purse for two tuppenny bits for the tickets, she said casually, 'Have you ever heard of someone called Madame Vichani, Ida?'

Ida looked blank. ''oo's she when she's at 'ome?'

'Oh, no one in particular,' Connie said airily. 'A dancing mistress I had once.' She could lie as well as Ida. If Ida *was* lying. 'Two to "British Museum", please.'

Ida was impressed by the Grecian-style pillars outside the museum. 'They look ancient and all.'

'They're fake old,' explained Connie. 'Just part of the architecture.'

How much more impressed Ida would be when she showed her what her parents had discovered in Egypt and donated to the museum! It made her feel proud and a little sad to show Ida the yellowing labels written in her father's neat elegant writing beside each scarab or fragment of pottery in the Egyptian Room.

But Ida wasn't impressed. 'They're very small.'

'My parents found them,' said Connie stiffly. 'They're thousands of years old.'

Ida saw Connie's face. 'Oh, I'm sorry. I was forgettin' you was an orphan, you poor kid. Like me.'

'You're not an orphan,' Connie said reprovingly. 'You have a mother.'

'So I do. Takes a lot of gettin' used to, you know.'

She recoiled from the mummies and said that the massive bull statue on the landing was very like Mr Thurston. They giggled about that.

However, she was much taken with the statues in the Greek Room. She prowled around them, open-mouthed.

'I never did! They've no clothes on!' She studied a fig leaf. 'Well, not much, anyhow.'

Connie left her there and went off on her own exploration.

When she grew up and became an anthropologist

would she visit Egypt or Greece first? Or would she venture to darkest Africa, where not nearly so much was known and she could become famous for some extraordinary discovery about early tribes? She would write up her research and then when she came back to London she would give lectures at the Royal Geographic Society and her audience would listen spellbound to the tales of her adventures. She would inspire other women to take up careers too.

Connie became aware that there was a disturbance in the hushed air of the Greek Room.

A bunch of young women were clustered round Ida as she admired the naked statues. They were listening to Ida's comments rather than those of the earnest bespectacled female, who was leading them around with a sheaf of notes in her hand.

'Nice legs,' Ida was musing and then venturing round the back of the statue, 'Oops, and there's 'is sit-upon. I never, and all on display like 'e 'adn't a care!'

'Isn't she just darling?'

'Utterly divino.'

'A true Cockney spirit!'

'I say, shall I ask her to my dance?' said one gleefully, her hair puffed out in the latest style beneath her wide ostrich-feathered hat. Her laugh trilled across the floor to Connie. 'What will Papa say?'

'Oh, you must. Oh, do. The Baron might even be her partner for a little dansare. She *is* very beautiful.'

'I say,' said the girl, advancing towards Ida. 'Do you have a card?'

Ida turned towards her blankly. 'Wot?'

'She doesn't know what a visiting card is, Marjorie.'

Connie decided to intervene. She marched up. 'Come on, Ida. We must go.'

'But I've not seen all the statues yet!' protested Ida.

'And who are you?' said the girl called Marjorie to Connie, looking highly amused. 'Are you her chaperone?'

More laughter rippled round the group.

'Yes,' said Connie fiercely. 'And I'm also her cousin, if you want to know.'

'Oh, I do,' said Marjorie. 'I want to ask her to my dance. It will be too, too frightfully amusing.'

'She doesn't want to go,' said Connie firmly.

'But I do,' said Ida.

'She doesn't go anywhere without me,' said Connie.

'You are a little young,' said Marjorie doubtfully, looking at Connie in her sailor dress. 'It's her mama who should come with her.'

Connie scowled at her and suddenly saw someone

she recognised in the group around her. The red hair was unmistakeable.

'I know who you are,' she said. 'You're the suffragette from Fuller's!'

The girl put her hand to her mouth in horror. She glanced at the older woman with the notes, but she had gathered up the rest of the girls and was ploughing on determindly with her interrrupted lecture, in a quiet spot, out of earshot.

'Please don't tell the press! My pater will be appalled and probably kick me out!'

There were murmurs of agreement amongst her friends. They clustered loyally around her.

'It will be the ruination of Lavender! She'll be disinherited!'

'Look!' said a tall girl, striding towards Ida. 'You can come to our dances if you say nothing.'

'Are you all having dances?' said Connie in bewilderment.

'It's the Season, silly!'

Ida needed no persuasion to give her name and address. Fortunately, none of them appeared to remember the newspaper stories about the little missing heiress called Ida Fairbanks: they had all been too young at the time.

Connie eventually dragged Ida away. She was furious, and cross with herself, too, for feeling so protective.

'You don't want to go to their stupid dances, do you? They'll just laugh at you! You won't know how to behave!'

'I don't mind,' said Ida simply. 'I've never bin to a dance. If you'd been stuck in an orphanage for years like I 'ave, then you'd want to go to dances too!'

They were going down the stairs in an unfriendly silence when Ida suddenly clutched Connie. She had gone even whiter than her usual pallor.

'It's 'im again,' she breathed. ''e's spyin' on me! Don't let 'im see me!'

Connie looked and there was the man with the stick, leaning against one of the pillars outside, smoking a cigarette. They could see him clearly through the open glass door.

She dragged Ida behind the bull statue on the landing.

'I thought you said you didn't know him!' she hissed.

'I don't,' whispered Ida. 'I saw 'im at the orphanage. 'E used to do odd jobs for Mrs Goodenough. I found out 'is name later: Leonard Crake. But when we saw 'im in Regent's Street I remembered 'im – when I thought about it after.'

'I think he recognised you,' said Connie. 'He was lying in wait for us. Just like he is now. He must have followed us here!'

Ida put her hands to her face. 'What can Leonard Crake want from me? I can't go back to the orphanage, Connie, I can't!'

8

Ida looked so alarmed that Connie couldn't help putting her arm round her.

'You're quite safe. You live in Alfred Place with us now.'

Ida nodded, but she didn't look reassured. They waited, pretending to examine the impressively muscular hind quarters of the bull for the benefit of the other visitors descending the stairs.

The man outside loitered, in no hurry to go. Every now and then he glanced into the museum through the glass doors and they shrank back behind the bull.

Eventually they heard the high-pitched chatter of Marjorie and her friends on their way out. They appeared to have discarded the female lecturer. Connie darted out and accosted Lavender, who seemed the most sensible of the girls.

'Can we join you? There's a man my cousin wants to avoid.'

'I say, how thrilling!' cried Lavender, her red hair ablaze. 'Down with all bounders! Gather together now, girls.'

So with Connie and Ida in their midst, the girls marched out.

Connie, peering between several expensively dressed bosoms, saw Leonard Crake stub out his cigarette on a pillar and turn away. A moment later he had disappeared behind the horse-drawn carriages drawn up beside the pavement.

'Was that him?' said Lavender, in Connie's ear. 'He looks a rogue.'

'I think he is,' said Connie.

Connie and Ida got off the train at South Kensington and were swept along to the lift with the other passengers. Connie happened to glance behind her and to her dismay saw Leonard Crake among the crowd.

They hadn't lost him after all.

He nipped in at the back of the lift as the gates clashed shut and she watched him out of the corner of her eye. It was difficult, being smaller than the majority of the other passengers – she had to look through the gaps between the briefcases and handbags and newspapers – but at least he couldn't see her watching him.

His face was sullen and closed, the cloth cap covering the flat back of his head. There was something stoat-like about him, she thought: his slight, wiry body, nimble in spite of the stick, and the way his head turned, his small, bold eyes searching the passengers in the lift.

She knew he was looking for Ida.

His gaze darted dangerously around until he saw her, standing tall, striking and unaware, close to the far gate.

Connie wormed her way towards Ida as the lift reached its first stop, the District line platform. The gate near them opened.

Connie pushed at Ida's back. 'Get out!' she hissed.

'Is this the right level?' said Ida, bewildered.

'Never mind! Get out now!'

Perhaps Ida accepted it as some childish game that Connie was playing, because she obeyed without more questions and they squeezed out before the gate was fully open.

'Run!' ordered Connie, grabbing her hand.

'What's the matter?' Ida gasped, as they dashed

along the tiled passage. In her long skirt she found it hard to keep up and somewhere Connie's hold on her slipped.

Connie was alone in a maze of smooth shiny tiles and Ida was nowhere to be seen.

She ran down the stairs to the District line platform, her heart thudding, and looked along the waiting passengers. No Ida. No Leonard Crake either, which was a relief.

She doubled back, racing up the stairs and along the passage to the lift. The waiting passengers stared and protested as Connie pushed through them and was first inside.

At the Piccadilly line level there was no sign of Ida, when Connie got out. She sped down the stairs and looked along the length of the Westbound platform first.

But when she ran through to the Eastbound platform she could see a forlorn figure waiting at the far end. Her head in one of the new hats was bent and she was staring at her feet.

'What are you doing?' Connie panted furiously.

'Waitin' for you,' said Ida pathetically. 'I didn't know where to go. Thought I was lost. They never let us out at the orphanage, see.'

'Leonard Crake was after you!' said Connie.

Ida put her hand to her mouth. 'What shall we do?'

'We have to go up to the ground level and get out!' said Connie.

But as they turned to go back to the lift, Leonard Crake emerged from one of the tunnels to the platform. Ida clutched Connie. They saw his head turn left and right. He began to tap towards them, rapidly and without limping. It struck Connie that he didn't carry the stick because he had a bad leg at all, but because it was useful in fights.

Then there was the distant rumble of a train approaching and a blast of hot steamy air. A crowd of people hurried through from another tunnel to catch it, and hid Leonard Crake from view.

'Come on!' said Connie.

She seized Ida's hand again and dragged her through the communicating tunnel to the Eastbound platform as the train rushed in behind them. There was a train waiting there, the doors open, and they jumped on, Ida holding on to her hat and looking frightened.

'Is 'e still there?'

'I think he's got on the other train,' said Connie, peering through the window. 'We're going to

Brompton Road now and not many passengers use it.'

The doors slid to behind them and they were enclosed in a fug of warmth and cigarette smoke. In a moment the train pulled out and they left the platform behind.

They came out of the station beside the Oratory, a large grey stone church on the Old Brompton Road. They were both breathing hard, but the huge lift to the ground level had been almost empty as it creaked upwards, and there was no sign of Leonard Crake.

'I think we've tricked him,' said Connie.

'Phew! That was a close one!' Ida said. There was the faint sheen of sweat on her otherwise perfect face.

Connie didn't like to remind her that Leonard Crake knew where she was living now. If he wanted to find her, he would.

'Tell me the truth, Ida,' she said sternly. 'There must be a reason that Crake is following you like this. He must have pursued us all the way to the British Museum as well! Did you run away from the orphanage?'

Ida shook her head, her blue eyes innocent. 'They wouldn't 'ave cared if I 'ad! Orphans are two a penny. Besides, I was too old to stay. They wanted me to get out – find a position somewhere.'

It was a mystery. Connie decided to forget it for the moment. They were definitely in need of refreshment. She steered Ida further up the Brompton Road, in search of the new Knightsbridge tea room, Richoux, near Cook's fishmongers.

'This is the life, eh?' said Ida, scraping up the last of the strawberry ice from her silvery goblet. ''ere I am, wiv a new mother, an aunt and a cousin. A whole family, 'cept for me dad and 'e couldn't 'elp dyin', could 'e, poor thing?' She leaned across the table confidentially. 'You know somethin'? The orphanage was near a boys' school – St Paul's, it was called – and every afternoon I used to look out of the dormitory winder and watch the young uns flyin' out to their mums or nurses, or whatever, and wish I could too.'

'And now you have,' said Connie. 'You've flown away. To us.'

'You're a right little pal, you are,' said Ida fondly, 'for all your funny ways – lookin' at dead long-ago things and that. What's the point in it?'

Connie looked at her earnestly across the small, round-topped table. 'One day I'm going to study real live people from around the world. This is preparation.'

Ida shook her head and licked her spoon. 'You

don't want to go travellin' to foreign places. Nasty germs. Dirt. Stay at 'ome and keep me company.'

A warm glow spread through Connie. They looked at each other and smiled.

The light caught the locket round Ida's neck and glinted on its new gold chain. 'May I see?' asked Connie, and Ida unfastened it and passed it across.

Connie turned it over in her hands. 'So pretty,' she said, and gave it back.

'Kept it safe all these years,' Ida said. 'It was the only thing I owned.' She leaned back and sighed. 'If I'm goin' to a dance, I'd better learn to speak like a toff smartish!'

'Don't,' said Connie fiercely. 'Don't change because of them. Stay as you are.'

But then she put her own spoon down thoughtfully.

Who exactly was Ida?

That was what she had to find out.

That evening, Connie turned to the page in her notebook headed 'Ida' and wrote a sub-heading.

New information:

Says she has not heard of Madame V. (?true/lie)

Frightened of L. Crake, odd-jobman at orphanage

because 1) he might make her go back? (unlikely)

2) another reason?

N.B. Ida's orphanage in H'smith was nr a boys' school called St Paul's

Her birthday is 29th July (arrival so close — is it SUSPICIOUS??)

9

In spite of Ida's worries about speaking 'like a toff', over the next few weeks her elocution lessons began to have the result that Aunt Dorothea desired, for Ida had a musical ear – as Arthur was always blushingly telling her.

If Ida had shown the slightest interest in Arthur, Connie might have disliked her a great deal for usurping her long-time confidant, but she did not. Indeed, Ida was turning out to be the perfect friend she had always wanted, even if she hadn't succeeded in interesting her in anthropology. There were times when Connie almost forgot that she should be investigating her.

Poor Arthur always looked downcast after Ida's singing lessons.

'Look at those grand invitations she's received,' he said dolefully to Connie, when they were alone in the drawing-room afterwards. He pointed to the mantelpiece where there were now two stiff cream cards, in writing that wasn't really writing at all but beautifully engraved print. 'She'll find a grand young man to match.'

'They'll all be cads,' Connie reassured him. 'Besides, Aunt Dorothea is going with her.' But secretly she didn't hold out many hopes for Arthur's prospects, nor for her timid and reclusive aunt's talents as a chaperone.

Ida had been having dancing lessons from jolly little Monsieur Jean, who only came up to Ida's chin and who, Connie had decided after close observation, wasn't really French at all but as English as she was. However, he had taught Ida how to waltz like a princess and do the latest Two-Step moves, the Rooster Strut and the Teddy Bears' Picnic.

Connie made Ida practise these with her, and they careered happily round the drawing-room together before a glum-faced Arthur. She wanted to make sure Ida was as prepared as possible for her grand new life. How Aunt Dorothea would cope with accompanying Ida to the dances, she wasn't sure. How much better it would be if she, Connie, could look after Ida!

Yet, mysteriously, Aunt Dorothea appeared to be looking forward to the prospect. She fingered the invitations and smiled, and ordered a new gown for herself from Lucile, the dressmakers.

On the evening of the first dance Connie watched Ida get ready.

At least there had been no sightings of Leonard Crake since his pursuit of Ida on the Underground. Whatever it was that he wanted from her, he must have decided to give up. That was odd, but a relief.

Ida, dressed in a pale green confection that made her look like a mermaid, was giving the mirror a satisfied smile when there was a commotion in the hall that came up the stairwell and through her open door.

'I'll go and see what's going on,' said Connie, who had become bored with all the endless preparations. She noticed, as she ran down, how threadbare the stair carpet had become, even in the last few months.

But she forgot about that as she saw that the hall was full of her two aunts, Mr Thurston, Martha – and a young man, whom she vaguely recognised. Mr Thurston was slapping his back and her aunts were kissing him delicately. He was tall and broad and muscular, with a tanned face and Mr Thurston's black hair, which on him looked somehow much more attractive.

She paused her headlong rush, to gather herself

73

together in a ladylike way. She was suddenly aware she must look like a schoolgirl, in her knee-length pinafore over her smock dress and the horrible black wool stockings, with the holes she had inked in so she needn't darn them.

Standing there, unnoticed for the moment, she was able to observe the various members of the household. Aunt Dorothea, already dressed for the dance, had tightened her lips and half turned away, while Aunt Sylvie was brimming with all the unusual excitement.

'We have had another visitor, you know, Frank – a visitor from the land of the dead,' she said breathlessly.

Frank looked at his father and their eyes met.

'You mean Ida?' said Frank cheerily. 'My father wrote me what happened, Sylvie. Can't wait to meet my long-lost relative!'

Connie stepped into the hall.

'She isn't actually your relative.' Everyone turned to her. 'Not your *blood* relative, that is.'

'Oh, Connie,' said Aunt Dorothea, hiding a smile. 'You do love being precise!'

'You remember my son Frank, don't you, Constance?' said Mr Thurston brusquely. 'He's come to visit us for a few weeks.'

Frank's dark eyes smiled at Connie. He was

extremely handsome. She had forgotten that, or perhaps she hadn't noticed before, three years ago. He had been working in the States and Canada ever since.

'My, how you've grown, little Connie Carew!' His voice had a soft twang. 'Not so little any more. Quite the young lady now. You'll have all the beaux after you!'

Connie stepped forward and held out her hand primly. 'Hello, Frank.'

'Heck, don't I deserve a kiss? Come here, you!'

She was lifted off her feet and twirled around, and then he planted a kiss on her cheek. For a second she felt his lips on her skin and then he had set her down. She felt a little dizzy.

'I want to hear all about your doings, Connie. Still want to be an an— What was it now?'

'An anthropologist.'

'Well now, aren't you something? And how's this great career of yours going?'

She couldn't tell if he was teasing her or not. She flushed and mumbled, 'Not awfully well.'

He took her hand. 'Come and tell me all about it, baby. And I'll tell you about the wild wild west!'

Connie was allowed to sit in the drawing-room on the first floor since it was Frank's first evening home.

Aunt Sylvie sat with them, murmuring to herself every now and then as was her habit – no one was ever sure whether she was listening to the conversation, or to a voice inside her head. Aunt Dorothea said she must go and see how Ida was getting on – they must leave shortly – and left them after a few minutes, but Mr Thurston stayed, taking up most of the sofa, slapping his great knees and chuckling every now and then, as yet another of Frank's extraordinary stories unfolded.

Connie listened, enthralled and flattered. Arthur didn't count – he was only a student still – but here was a young man, who must be in his twenties at least, paying her attention. She was going to tell him all about her plans for the future.

But as the minutes passed, it became clear that Frank wasn't much interested in Connie's career, after all. His own was far more exciting. And he clearly loved having an admiring audience.

Mr Thurston and Frank were between them getting

through a good deal of the sherry in the decanter when the door opened and Ida swept into the room in her ball gown.

She put her hand to her mouth. 'I didn't know you had a guest, Harold. I wanted to say goodbye to – Aunt Sylvie.' She hesitated, as if the words were still unfamiliar, before she bent and kissed her.

Aunt Sylvie came out of her reverie. 'You look magnificent, my dear.' She put her old hand on Ida's smooth bare shoulder. 'Be careful,' she whispered.

Both men had risen to their feet, Mr Thurston, with a grunt, and Frank, with alacrity. He gazed at the vision before him – piled up pale gold hair and long sea-green dress – and held out his hand.

'Frank Thurston at your service, mam. Pleased to meet you, I'm sure.'

Ida took his tanned hand in her newly unblemished, pampered white one.

'*How do you do?*' she said carefully.

So that was that. Frank's whole attention was now concentrated on Ida. Mr Thurston watched them with glazed eyes from his sofa and downed more sherry and Aunt Sylvie smiled vaguely and continued a background murmuring, like the sound of the sea.

Connie was ignored. She sat in her chair by the

unlit grate as the evening deepened and Martha came in to light the gas lamps.

A lump of resentment grew heavy in her chest. She stared at her feet in their button boots and glowered.

Ida had belonged to her so far – she was her cousin (possibly) and special friend – but she had no time for Connie now. Her head was quite turned by Frank, who had arrived suddenly out of the blue with his handsome looks and beguiling stories. Earlier, he had seemed to think Connie was the ideal listener. But within moments of Ida's arrival, he had forgotten she existed.

Aunt Sylvie left first, muttering under her breath, words that made no sense to Connie.

Shortly afterwards she slipped out herself, unnoticed by the other three, and began to stump up the stairs to her bedroom on the top floor. She felt thoroughly ruffled by the evening.

She reached the third landing and paused. Ida's bedroom door was half open and she could hear someone moving about inside. The daylight was fading early after an overcast day and the landing was shadowy. Martha had not been up here yet to light the gas. The noises continued, as if someone were pacing about inside the room.

Connie hesitated and a prickle went down her spine. Despite the rational, scientific person she knew herself to be, she suddenly wondered if it might be the ghost of the real little Ida come back to haunt them for taking in the girl downstairs.

She listened again. No, these footsteps were not made by the small, stubby feet of a two-year-old but the heavy ones of a grown-up.

She pushed the door fully open and went in.

'Aunt Sylvie! What are you doing in here?'

Her aunt turned to her, her gaze distracted, the whites of her eyes shining in the gloom. 'It's a warning!' she hissed.

'What is?'

Her aunt pointed dramatically to a picture hanging lopsidedly on the wall, then to a chair lying on its side on the floor, a jumble of Ida's underclothes – combinations, liberty bodice and garters – scattered around it. 'You see?' she said triumphantly.

'Ida's made a mess, that's all. She never had a nanny who scolded her for being untidy.'

Aunt Sylvie shook her head so that her wig slipped further askew than ever. 'No, dear. It's evil vibrations in the air. They're in this house. I can feel them. They're a warning.'

'A warning about what, Aunt Sylvie?' Connie was used to her aunt's periods of madness, but in the dim hush of the room the whispered words held an authority and menace. She felt suddenly chilled.

'They're out to harm her.'

'Who are?'

Her aunt pressed her lips together and looked away. 'I mustn't tell,' she said at last.

'Is it the man with the stick?' said Connie urgently. 'Is it Leonard Crake?' But how would her aunt know him?

'I've heard her crying in the night. I've seen her face in the mirror.'

'Who are you talking about, Aunt Sylvie?'

'Why, little Ida, of course,' her aunt said impatiently, forgetting to whisper. 'Little Ida Fairbanks.'

Connie frowned. 'But she's downstairs. She's come back. She's grown up now, not little any more.'

Aunt Sylvie looked confused. She clutched Connie's sleeve. 'She's in danger. Little Ida's in deadly danger. You must stop them, Connie!'

10

It took Connie a while to calm Aunt Sylvie down, she became so agitated. Eventually, she managed to persuade her aunt to leave and go to her own bedroom across the landing. Connie shut the door on her firmly and bumped into Martha.

'My aunt's having one of her turns,' explained Connie.

'Oh, is she?' Martha, unconcerned, put a match to the gas. She was as used to Aunt Sylvie's bouts of battiness as Connie. 'I'll bring her up some hot milk in a bit. That usually settles her.' She put a hand on her stout hip and rubbed it. 'Wish Mr Thurston would put in electricity. Save me climbing all these stairs every night!'

She went into Ida's bedroom, lit the lamp and turned it low. 'Gracious, what a mess!' she exclaimed, looking around.

'I'll tidy it, Martha,' said Connie.

'You're a good girl, Miss Constance.' She paused and shook her head. 'You can't make a silk purse out of a soused herring however hard you try, that's what I say!'

Connie heard Martha's heavy feet go back down the stairs. Was Ida the soused herring? she wondered, puzzled.

In the warm, yellow light Martha had left behind Connie straightened the picture and stood the chair up again, putting Ida's underclothes in a heap on the seat. On Ida's dressing-table there were speckles of face-powder, a Guerlain scent bottle with its top off and a pot of lip salve which would dry out if left open. The mess had definitely been made by Ida's very human hand.

Connie looked around quickly, just in case, but the room looked quite ordinary in the gaslight. It still smelled faintly of lavender and vanilla, Ida's perfume, which competed with the more pungent smell of recently lit gas and still-warm curling tongs. She dabbed a little *Jicky* behind her ears and put the top back on the bottle, then smeared some lip salve on her mouth and pouted at herself in the mirror. She would never look as beautiful as Ida, even with glossy lips.

She was experimenting with the powder puff when she heard steps coming up the stairs, light and quick. She straightened guiltily and just had time to put the puff down and face the door, when Ida burst in, clutching her long dress up in either hand in a very unladylike manner and breathing hard.

She stopped her headlong rush and stared at Connie.

'What are you doin' in here all on your own?'

'Nothing,' said Connie, almost truthfully. 'I was tidying up. You left an awful pickle.'

'You shouldn't enter other people's rooms without their permission,' said Ida grandly. A thought seemed to strike her. 'You was – *were* – spyin', wasn't you? That was it. Own up.'

'I was not!' said Connie hotly.

It occurred to her too late that that was what she should have been doing, instead of playing with Ida's cosmetics. She should have been looking for some incriminating evidence about Ida's identity. 'You're not hiding anything, are you, Ida?' she added innocently. 'So why should I spy on you?'

Ida came closer and narrowed her blue eyes. 'You're the only one who don't believe me, that's why!'

83

'What do you mean?'

This made Ida crosser still. 'You know very well. Everyone else – me mother and aunt and even Mr Thurston – they all believe that I'm the lost child from long ago. But you – my little cousin – you don't believe it, do you?'

Connie said nothing. She couldn't lie about it: she simply didn't know. She stared at the floorboards miserably.

'I thought you were my chum,' said Ida.

'I am, I am!'

'No, you're not, not if you don't believe me. What kind of friend is that? You think you're clever and know the truth!'

Connie shook her head miserably. 'I'm sorry, Ida. I didn't mean—'

'You're so sharp you'll cut yourself one day, Connie Carew! Search all you like, but you'll not find nothin'!'

Ida turned away and snatched up a beaded evening bag from the bed. 'Lumme, I'm goin' to be late,' she muttered to herself.

She held the door open for Connie. 'Now, go! And never, *ever*, spy on me again, do you hear?'

Connie walked out, trying to look dignified, but her

mouth was trembling. She heard Ida's footsteps die away down the stairs as she trudged up through the darkness to her own room.

11

The next day was Friday, which was the day Arthur came to teach Piano.

Ida had not appeared at breakfast. She had come in very late, Martha informed Connie, and was 'sleeping it off'.

Connie was relieved not to see her. She thought Aunt Dorothea might be 'sleeping it off' too, so she didn't go and visit her for a report on the dance. She ate her own breakfast alone, since Mr Thurston and Frank had already had theirs and were closeted together in Mr Thurston's study. As she stuffed her toast crusts behind the sideboard, she could hear their raised voices and wondered briefly what they were arguing about.

Arthur looked very cast down by Ida's absence.

'She was doing so splendidly at "Chopsticks",' he said mournfully.

Halfway through the lesson, Ida popped her head round the door. Colour had come into her cheeks while she had been at Alfred Place; she looked pinkly blooming, as if she hadn't been up half the night.

'Frank is takin' me out to luncheon, so I'll miss today's lesson. You don't mind, Arthur dear?'

When she had gone, Arthur subsided on to a chair and put his head in his hands. 'Who is Frank?'

'Her step-cousin,' said Connie. 'He's come to stay. If you want to win Ida, you'll have to fight for her.'

'I'm only her music tutor.'

'She called you "dear".'

'It doesn't mean anything with her,' he said despairingly. 'You know it doesn't.'

Connie twisted round on the piano stool and eyed him sternly.

'Don't be such a milk-sop, Arthur! Now, is Ida the only girl for you?'

Arthur blinked. 'Well, yes, I suppose she is. Yes, absolutely.'

'Then in that case we have got to do something!'

There was alarm in Arthur's dreamy eyes. 'What sort of something?'

'We've got to find out who she really is. If she is Ida Fairbanks or an imposter, out to steal the Fairbanks fortune. That would make her a criminal.'

'Oh, I say! Not really! Not Ida!'

'She may not be "Ida" at all, don't you see? She may be deceiving us all – you, too. And we haven't got long – her birthday's at the end of next month! That's when she'll get the inheritance. Wouldn't it be better to find out now, rather than later? That is, if you have serious intentions?'

'Oh, I do. Absolutely. Need to be able to trust her, you're right.' He scratched his curly head. 'But why do *you* want to find out?'

Connie hesitated. 'I want to believe she is my cousin. It's important.'

'I see,' mused Arthur. 'It will be pretty rotten for Mrs T, too, if it turns out that Ida isn't her daughter.'

'So you'll help me, then? That is,' she added, watching his face, 'if you care about Ida enough.'

'Oh, I do!' He blushed furiously. 'She's the bee's knees, isn't she, even if she is a criminal?' He added, with a sigh, 'But I suppose I'd better find out the truth.'

Connie leaped from the stool and planted a kiss on his surprised cheek. 'You're a brick, Arthur! I've always known that!'

'But how are we going to do it, Connie?'

The night before, Connie had looked at her list of questions concerning Ida and decided that the easiest one to to pursue might be *Habitat: formerly an orphanage (?) in Hammersmith, W. London.*

The orphanage would be able to give her some information, Connie was sure. She would be able to check whether Ida's story was true. And an orphanage couldn't be too difficult to find. She imagined a large house bursting with noisy children, happy to have a home even if they didn't have parents.

But what if the dreadful-sounding Mrs Goodenough decided that she, Connie, was a handy replacement for Ida and decided to keep her there to look after the little ones? She was an orphan, too, after all. Perhaps she should take someone with her. An accomplice.

Who better than Arthur?

No one saw them leave the house.

Ida and Frank had already gone for their luncheon, Mr Thurston had long departed for goodness knows where, the aunts were upstairs closeted together – perhaps discussing the dance – and Miss Poots wouldn't arrive until the afternoon.

They shut the door of the drawing-room behind them so Martha would think they were still in there and wouldn't go in, and Connie crammed on her hat.

As they crossed the Cromwell Road, the police were putting out barriers for the opening of the new arched façade of the Victoria and Albert Museum by the King and Queen; already people were gathering in the drizzle to watch.

They walked up towards Kensington Gore, past the enticing museums of Exhibition Road, their edges soot-stained as if a giant hand was trying to erase them with a dirty India rubber. It was a pity, thought Connie, that the only clean buildings in London were the boring, pompous ones with stiffly starched fronts that had been recently built in Holborn, Whitehall and the West End.

'Do you actually know where we're going?' enquired Arthur, unfurling his black umbrella and holding it over Connie gallantly, as they left the Science and Natural History Museums behind them.

'We have to find St Paul's School,' said Connie.

'I know where that is now. It's on the Hammersmith Road. I looked it up in the telephone directory. Ida said the orphanage was near there. She used to watch the boys going home.'

'But we can't just march into the orphanage, can we?'

'I'll think of an excuse while we're on the Hammersmith omnibus,' said Connie.

The omnibus smelled of tobacco smoke and damp overcoats. Connie peered out of the smeary window, as the grander houses and shops of Kensington High Street gave way to the smaller, narrower shops of Hammersmith Road. It was easy to spot the school, an imposing Victorian building with several pointed towers, set back from the road.

They pulled the bell-rope for the next stop and climbed out.

Connie looked around. There was no building anywhere that might be a large orphanage. Her heart sank. Perhaps Ida had made it all up. But her comment about the boys going home to their families had had the ring of truth.

'It must be up a side street nearby,' she said to Arthur.

They went down a couple of streets of mean, sooty little houses. The air was sticky with the drizzle, the sky whitish all over, like one of Cook's mixing bowls. Ragged, barefoot children played in the muddy gutters, their hair plastered to their heads, their faces thin and filthy. They stared at Connie in her clean clothes and Arthur with his umbrella. It was very different from the shining white houses of Thurloe Square and the cosseted children with their nursemaids, playing in the leafy garden of the square.

Mr Asquith and his government should do something for children like these! thought Connie indignantly.

At last, in a street almost opposite the school, they found what they were looking for. It was halfway down: two grimy houses, larger than the others, leaning together behind a brick wall. A peeling notice-board outside read *The Sisters of Hope: Home for Destitute Children*. But it looked completely without hope, the most dismal place Connie had ever seen, and seemed deserted, with no sign of any movement behind the iron gates.

'Is this it?' said Arthur.

'You couldn't possibly see the school from here,' said Connie, puzzled. But Ida hadn't made it up, not quite. She must have seen the boys coming out at the end of the school day – perhaps when the orphans were taken for a walk – and envied them.

As if to illustrate this, the gates were suddenly opened by a pinch-faced woman, and a crocodile of little girls and boys holding hands walked out hesitantly, led by two older girls. They came past Connie and Arthur, and Connie looked into their faces. They were dull-eyed and without expression, for all that they were clean and reasonably clothed. They were completely silent. The woman walked behind, flapping at them with her bony hands, as if she was shooing on a herd of small animals.

The gates had been left open.

'Come on,' said Connie, as soon as the sad little troupe had turned into Hammersmith Road. She pulled Arthur through the gates into the weedy rectangle in front of the orphanage. 'Remember your story, Arthur?'

He bit his lip. 'It's a lie, Connie.'

'A white lie. We've got to find out the truth, remember?'

All the same, she had to pull him up the steps. The

93

front door of the nearest house seemed to be the main entrance and it was still slightly open. Connie pushed against it and dragged Arthur inside with her.

They found themselves in a dark narrow hallway, with rooms off to one side and a shadowy staircase at the end. The acid smell of bleach in the confined space caught in Connie's throat. From above came the high sound of children's voices and a harsh voice quietening them.

'I bet that's Mrs Goodenough,' whispered Connie.

Arthur folded his umbrella back into its neat creases with care. He looked very unhappy. 'What do we do now?'

For answer Connie turned the handle of the nearest door quietly and peered round it. She beckoned to Arthur without speaking and he joined her reluctantly.

Connie knocked. Then, without waiting for an answer, she marched straight in.

12

They were in a small stuffy office, its dirty windows closed, its furniture meagre. A middle-aged man was crouched in a sagging armchair, reading the *Daily Mail*, its headlines shouting in large black letters: '**Serialisation Starts Today: Germany To Invade England!**'

His grey face was tired and careworn behind his spectacles. Behind him were shelves of files bulging with papers and, on a table next to a typewriting machine, more files were balanced precariously on top of each other.

The man looked up and frowned. 'Who are you?' he said wearily. 'How did you get in?'

'We're so sorry to disturb you, sir, but the front door was open,' said Connie politely.

'In Records we don't usually see anyone without an appointment.'

That sounded very grand for so dilapidated a place. Connie came forward and put on her most winning smile. 'I realise how busy you must be, sir, but we have a query, my brother and I.'

The man put down his newspaper and stared at her, pushing his spectacles up on his nose. His face was kind, Connie thought, but startled, as if he didn't get many visits from twelve-year-old girls.

She prodded Arthur. He stood, opening and shutting his mouth as if he had forgotten what he was meant to say.

'We think,' said Connie, quickly filling in the gap, 'that a long-lost relative of ours may have been taken in here as a baby.'

The man considered her, from the beribboned hat on her ringlets down to her laced leather shoes, polished by Martha that morning. 'A relation of yours, miss? I doubt it.'

'We have it on good authority that she did live here until very recently. Couldn't you look her up in your records?' Connie waved her arm at the files. 'I'm sure she must be entered somewhere. We want to trace her and welcome her back into the family. I think,' she added, gazing at him persuasively, 'that you may even remember her yourself, sir.'

The man grunted. 'What was her name?'

'Ida – Ida Brown.'

'Ida.' The man smiled and his whole face lightened. ''Course I remember her. A beautiful child, who grew into a lovely young lady. We just called her Ida. Don't believe she had a surname. When she was older she helped out with the little ones. It was a shame when she left at sixteen but we can't keep them for ever. Too expensive.'

'Sixteen?' said Connie, taken aback.

The man nodded. 'That's how old we reckoned she was. Usually they have to go at fourteen, but we made an exception in her case. 'Bout a year ago she left. I can check the date for you if you like.'

Connie gulped. She didn't look at Arthur.

'Please, sir. If you would.'

Without leaving his armchair, the man reached across to the table and eased out a newish-looking file from the pile, as if he knew exactly where he had put each one. This was labelled 'Departures '08'. He put it on his knee with great deliberation, fixed his spectacles more securely round his ears and seemed to take an eternity thumbing through the index.

'No surname, see,' he said at one point, as explanation. 'Have to look through the 'No Names' section. Most children go straight on to the local workhouse. The likely ones get apprenticeships if they're lucky. The girls may get taken on as domestics, paid a pittance, then killed with hard work. The women that come here looking for cheap labour –' he pursed his lips '– let's say there's no way I'd send a child to work for them. I think that's what happened to your Ida.'

Connie shook her head. There was the beginning of a lump in her throat and she couldn't speak. Ida hadn't told them the truth. Where had she been for the last year?

'Ah, here we are,' said the man, a trace of complacency in his tone. 'I can usually answer every query I receive regarding our children.'

He read out: 'Ida. No surname registered on arrival 1894. Approximate age: two years.' He nodded at Connie. 'It's in Mrs Goodenough's handwriting. She's our matron.'

So the child had arrived when she was two, the same age as Ida had been when she went missing.

'Does it say anything else about her arrival?' Connie said urgently. 'About a locket she was wearing?'

The man frowned. 'Hang on a mo, will you, miss? Thought it was her leaving date you wanted. Arrivals are another batch of files altogether.' He paused and looked up at her with a faint smile. 'But I do remember Ida's arrival. Don't need a file to tell me. I'd just started working here, see? I wasn't doing the registers then, just helping out. But the story was that she'd been found curled up in a banana crate on our doorstep.'

So that at least was true.

'What about the locket with her name on it?'

The man shook his head. 'I don't know anything about a locket. "No possessions" it says here.'

'Then why was she called Ida?'

'She was always chattering, I think that was why. "Ida do dis, Ida do dat" – she was probably just saying "I" but we called her Ida anyway.'

He gave a reminiscent smile. 'I watched her grow up into the prettiest little thing. You lose your heart to some of them. And there was something about Ida that made you want to protect her. You didn't want any harm to come to her, know what I mean? She was so fragile and perfect.'

He sighed. 'It's good to know she had a good family all along. I always thought she was a cut above.' He looked accusingly at Arthur. 'Though you've taken your time about tracing her, haven't you, young man?'

Arthur shuffled his feet and went pink. 'It's not that—' he began.

Connie interrupted before Arthur could ruin their story. 'But Ida left here a year ago? Are you sure?'

The man pushed his spectacles down on his nose and read out, 'Departed Sisters of Hope 30 June 1908.'

'Does it say where she went?'

'Hold on, miss. You are the impatient one, aren't you? The same can't be said for your brother –' he gave Arthur a disparaging glance '– more's the pity.'

His finger traced the handwritten words.

'Employer's name: Mrs Brown of Pelham Crescent, SW.' He looked up at Connie and smiled. 'A good address, little miss. She's been well looked after there, I'm sure you'll find. Mrs Brown is a friend of Mrs Goodenough, our head matron.'

Connie cleared her throat. 'Thank you very much, sir,' she managed to say. 'You've been most helpful.'

She prodded Arthur and they left the man to his newspaper. But at the doorway Connie paused and pulled herself together.

'I don't suppose, sir,' she said, 'you know a Mr Leonard Crake?'

The man's benign expression altered. 'He's done

odd jobs for us. I wouldn't trust him further than I could spit a pip, begging your pardon, miss. How in heaven's name do you know him?'

'I don't, not really,' said Connie.

When she turned to leave, there was a large woman blocking the doorway. She wore a stiffly starched matron's cap and could only be Mrs Goodenough. Arthur trod painfully on Connie's heels as Connie backed away.

The woman's face looked like a ball of suet. Out of it a small, puckered mouth moved and spoke, in the same hard voice that Connie had heard before.

'Trouble, Mr Crabb?'

'No trouble at all, Mrs Goodenough,' the man said hastily.

The woman's button eyes flicked down to Connie, registered that she was merely a child and not worth her attention, then over to Arthur in his shabby clothes. Her mean little mouth curled disdainfully.

'Who are these two, Mr Crabb?'

'The young lady and gentleman are sister and brother, Mrs Goodenough,' gabbled Mr Crabb. He didn't look at her but busied himself with putting the file away in the right place. He was frightened of her, Connie realised.

'They are relations of Ida, the young girl who left us some while ago, you remember, Mrs Goodenough? The girl you kept on because you said she was so helpful. They wanted to know her current whereabouts so they can find her.'

His voice rose higher as Mrs Goodenough came over to his desk and loomed over him.

'And what are their names, Mr Crabb? You have made a note of them, I take it?'

The doorway was clear. As Mrs Goodenough turned her pudding face to them again, Connie grabbed Arthur's hand and pulled him out of the room.

'Now, wait a minute!' she heard Mrs Goodenough shout after them. 'I need your names, you and your brother!'

Connie and Arthur sat glumly side by side in the omnibus on the way back.

'What a horror that woman was!' said Arthur.

'No wonder Ida hated her,' said Connie.

Neither of them could speak yet of what really mattered. The streets outside were grey and dismal with the falling rain. Connie was thinking hard, trying to swallow the lump of disappointment in her throat. Her beautiful new cousin – she had so wanted to believe in her.

At last Arthur said, 'What does it mean, Connie?'

He looked bewildered, his eyes full of hurt, as if he realised his beloved wasn't quite what he had thought. But he looked at Connie as if he relied on her for an answer that would make everything all right.

Connie couldn't give that.

'I'm afraid Ida lied to us, Arthur. She didn't come straight from the orphanage. She's spent the last year in Pelham Crescent!'

He wrinkled his brow. 'Are you going to tell your aunt?'

'Not yet. I want to be sure first. We need more proof. I think I know which house it is in Pelham Crescent and who "Mrs Brown" is. You remember the séance I told you about? I bet Madame Vichani and Mrs Brown are the same person!'

'Does that mean Ida is an imposter?'

'I don't know. Her story about being left at the orphanage was true. But we've got to find out why Ida hasn't told us where she's been for the last year.'

'Can't we ask her?'

'No, you duffer! She mightn't tell us the truth. Besides, we don't want to put her on her guard. We've got to do more research.'

Arthur's face fell. He hated subterfuge and was clearly no good at detecting. 'What do you mean by "more research?"' he asked warily.

'We have to investigate Madame Vichani.'

'How do we do that?'

'We must attend a séance, Arthur.'

As they walked down Exhibition Road Connie had a strange feeling that they were being followed. Yet every time she looked behind her there was no figure lurking behind one of the soot-stained pillars that lined the road.

When they reached the Cromwell Road it was to find it blocked with waggons, hansom-cabs and motorised vehicles. There was a tremendous noise of hooting and stalled engines, mixed with the neighing of frightened horses and the clatter of hooves on the wet road. People surged against the barriers, hoping to catch a glimpse of the King and Queen as they arrived at the Victoria and Albert Museum.

Connie looked for a way to cross through the commotion.

'Can I help you, miss?' said a policeman. 'Trying to get over the road, are you?'

When she had been escorted safely through the traffic to the pavement on the other side she looked around for Arthur. Surely he'd followed her? She couldn't see him anywhere, not that it was easy, given how many people there were and most of them a good deal taller than she was. She was squashed by bodies on every side.

She felt a hand on the shoulder of her coat. She looked around with relief, thinking it must be Arthur. But she looked into the small, sharp eyes of Leonard Crake.

'A word with you, miss.'

Her heart began to hammer. She wrenched away, but the hand on her shoulder gripped her. The people around her were oblivious, their attention fixed on the waiting space in front of the museum.

'What do you want?' she stammered.

'I want you to stop interfering,' Crake hissed in her ear. 'Don't poke your nose into things you know nothing about. Keep out of this business!' His grip tightened painfully. 'I'm warning you!'

And then his hand left her shoulder and he vanished into the crowd, as people surged forward shouting 'Bertie! Bertie!' and a cheer went up.

'Hello, Connie,' said Arthur, squeezing his gangling frame between two portly men, his umbrella still intact and folded carried before him like a totem pole. 'Thought I'd lost you.'

13

That night it seemed to Connie that the damp patch in her bedroom had grown more defined: a huge face glaring down at her from the crooked angles of the ceiling. It had developed a Nose now. The measles rash had spread, multiplying darkly on the walls against the pitted paper and gathering around her bed.

'I am a practical person,' she told herself. 'It's only condensation.'

All the same she had not wanted to blow out her candle until Martha came at last to bed, shaking the landing with the tired tramp of her feet and later, with her snoring in the bedroom next door.

Connie filled in the time by writing in her notebook.

Plan of Action
Aim: discover who Ida is (before 29th July)

1. Investigate orphanage (with a feeling of triumph she was able to put a large tick beside this)

2. Investigate Madame Vichani

It was a rather short list, she thought doubtfully, but perhaps some other points would occur to her after she and Arthur had been to another séance.

The next séance would be held on the following Wednesday afternoon. That morning Connie came down to breakfast early.

Ida had been to her second ball the night before and must be 'sleeping it off' again, and Aunt Dorothea's bedroom door had been firmly shut when she passed it. Connie was alone in the morning-room, the long table laid with its white cloth and the silver covers put over the food on the sideboard as usual. Pale sunlight reached in tentatively through the long windows.

The post had come already and beside Mr Thurston's place at the table was a pile of envelopes.

Connie glanced at them as she passed on her way to the sideboard to help herself to kidneys and bacon, and noticed the name of his club with the St James's address stamped on the top envelope. A bill, probably. Perhaps they were all bills; it was nearly the end of the month.

On impulse, because she never had any post herself, she began to look through the other envelopes. One was stamped with a Savile Row address below the name, one with a name and address in Old Bond Street (both Mr Thurston's tailors, she thought), then there was a plain buff one addressed to Mr Thurston in typewriting, without any sender's name on it at all.

She was about to investigate further when Martha came in, carrying two morning newspapers. She looked at Connie in surprise as she jumped guiltily away from the post.

'Why, Miss Constance, you were so quiet I thought no one was in here!'

She was whispering, which was odd since usually Martha had a loud, cheerful voice. She put the papers down on the sideboard, turned around and wrung her hands.

'It's a bad business,' she muttered. 'Don't know what the Master will say!'

'What's the matter, Martha?'

'Look, Miss Constance!'

She came closer and opened out one of the papers past the front page of advertisements.

There was a long item headed by large black letters:

Missing Heiress Returns After Fifteen Years!
First Public Appearance Of Miss Ida Fairbanks

Last night the lavish dance given by Lady Ponsonby for the coming-out of her debutante daughter, the Honorable Marjorie Ponsonby, was attended by a beautiful mystery guest. She was later announced as none other than Miss Ida Fairbanks, who has been living incognito at her old home in Alfred Place West, South Kensington, for the past few weeks. Her remarkable reappearance after so many years remains unexplained.'

Connie glanced down further. 'Years without hope . . . Miss Fairbanks due to inherit considerable fortune . . . 18th birthday imminent . . .'

'Mrs Thurston wanted to keep it quiet, I know,' moaned Martha. 'She had enough of them journalists at the time. She told us servants not to say a word after Miss Ida's return in case it got into the newspapers. Miss Ida must have been spotted at that dance. I don't know why the press was there, I'm sure.'

'I believe I do,' said Connie, for on the same page another item was headed

Lady Lavender Lamont joins the Suffragettes!
Father's Fury! Dramatic Scene at Society Dance!

'And now the press have traced Miss Ida here,' hissed Martha, in a stage whisper. She pointed to the window. 'It's like bees to the honeypot!'

Connie went over to the window and peered down. She understood why Martha was whispering now. On the pavement outside there was a cluster of journalists, with notebooks and large cameras on tripods.

She half drew the curtains but someone had already seen her. There was a flurry of excitement as faces turned towards her and she backed away hurriedly.

She was sitting down again to finish her breakfast when Mr Thurston and Frank came in. Mr Thurston was scowling beneath his oiled black hair; Frank looked dapper and sleek, his tanned face shining.

'It's our only hope, Frank! You've got to do it!'

'I'll do my best, Pa.'

They broke off when they saw Connie and Martha. Martha gave a little bob and took herself off. The door closed.

'Good morning,' said Connie demurely.

Mr Thurston grunted and Frank gave her a token grin, his teeth flashing white.

Indeed, when they had helped themselves at the sideboard and sat down they appeared to forget about her altogether, careless of what they were saying in front of her – or perhaps they simply assumed that whatever they said would go above her head. Connie was quite used to that, with grown-ups.

At the other end of the table she sat silently, chewing her toast which, as always, had been left out in the silver rack too long, and listened, her head bent.

'You see?' Mr Thurston gathered up his post in one broad hand and flourished it at Frank. 'That's why! And you're in trouble too, son, don't tell me you're not. I know how many shares you hold. And you encouraged me to buy!'

Frank sounded sulky. 'It seemed a good prospect at the time. In my position—'

His father snorted. 'Your position! You wouldn't have bought that company without my help. I knew the right person, that's why. And now all my contacts are running away from me, running scared because you –' he pointed a thick finger at Frank '– have made a right bosh of it over in the States. And we're losing money hand over fist.'

'I'm sorry, Pa.'

'Well, you know what you've got to do.'

'It would help if you stopped your gambling,' muttered Frank sullenly. His father affected not to hear but they both suddenly seemed aware of Connie.

'Let's have a dekko at those newspapers, then,' said Mr Thurston in a hearty tone, pushing his plate to one side.

Didn't he know what was going on outside? Perhaps he thought the curtains had been drawn against the morning's sun. But Connie was interested to hear his reaction. Very interested.

Mr Thurston opened his paper out. He must see the item now. Connie found she was clenching her hands, waiting for his rage.

He stabbed the paper with a finger. 'See this, son?'

Frank craned over and nodded. 'So it's come out in the press at last.'

'A little word on the telephone last night,' Mr Thurston said, a note of smugness in his voice. 'That's all it took. Now I must get Dorothea to pose with her outside so they can take pictures.'

Connie hid her astonishment. So Mr Thurston himself had told the newspapers about Ida! She had expected him to be angry about the intrusion of their privacy, but he was the cause of it. As they both pored over the article she slipped out of the room without excusing herself. Neither of the men looked up.

'You know what this means, don't you?' Mr Thurston was saying. 'Every Tom, Dick and Harry will be after her now. You'd better get a move on, Frank!'

Connie thought Ida might still be asleep after the dance but as she reached the third landing she heard the sound of sobs coming from behind her bedroom door.

She hesitated, torn. There were so many strange and unresolved questions about Ida. And besides, she had been threatened herself by the vile Leonard Crake. But after a moment she could bear it no longer and knocked on the door.

When she didn't get a reply she opened the door cautiously and looked in.

Ida was sitting up in bed in her nightie, a newspaper spread over her knees and her breakfast tray untouched on the floor, next to some crumpled and sodden handkerchiefs.

She looked up and glared. Her eyes looked even more beautiful when filled with tears. 'Go 'way!' she said snuffily.

'I wanted to let you know – no one's cross about it.' Connie gestured at the newspaper. 'Mr Thurston – he seems pleased.'

'Pleased! It was right horrible, I tell you, Connie! I never want to go to another beastly dance in me life!'

'I haven't even been to even one yet,' said Connie humbly. 'Can you tell me about it?'

Ida glowered at her, but the impulse to unburden herself of the previous evening's horrors was clearly too much to resist. She patted her bed with pretend reluctance. 'Sit down, then.'

Connie sat and listened.

Ida sniffed. 'I never would have done it – tell all London who I am, I mean – but at the Hon Marjorie's they had this right posh gov'nor giving out names as we came in. I was half minded to say "Ida Brown" but then I thought I'm not her any more, might as well say it like it is, and I knew it would please Mother. So I said "Ida Fairbanks" straight out and he – that man – repeated it in a big voice like you never heard before and these old ladies, gossiping round the edge of the ballroom, they all sat up and stared at me and Mother!'

'How beastly for you for you both,' said Connie sympathetically, and she meant it. Shy Aunt Dorothea must have hated it!

'And after that it was perfeckly dreadful. I had all these young lads egged on by their mamas to ask me to dance, wanting to have a go with me round the floor, and Mother tellin' me I should. I was surrounded by them, I tell you! I filled me dance card right up, quite wore out the pencil stub. And there was one who kept asking questions. I think he was a journalist.'

'So what happened then? What about Lady Lavender?'

'I shouldn't say this, but I tell you, Connie, if it hadn't been for her pa storming in and dragging her off for a dressing-down, I never would have escaped. We got away while all them journalists were clustered round outside, waiting for her. They didn't recognise me face when I came out and Mother's neither.'

'You mustn't let them photograph you. I'll see if I can put them off the scent.'

'Oh, would you, Connie? You're the tops, I'll say that. Sorry I was cross last night.'

'Stay inside today,' urged Connie.

Ida put her hands to her hair, which was tightly done up in curling rags. 'But I'm meant to be having a walk with Frank, this afters.'

'Then go out through the back garden, into the mews,' said Connie. 'If you must.'

She looked at Ida's little jewelled clock on the bedside table. It was almost time for Miss Poots to arrive for the morning's lessons.

'I'll see what I can do about those newspaper men,' she said quickly, and ran down the stairs before Martha could open the front door to her governess.

Miss Poots arrived in a fluster.

Connie knew when she had arrived because the noise outside became pandemonium. Hardly had she knocked, than Connie opened the door and she almost fell into the hall.

'Oh, those dreadful men! Lurking around outside like that, asking me questions about Ida. Whoever are they? They can't be her *suitors*, surely?'

'They're from the newspapers,' said Connie. 'I'll

explain everything in a minute, Pootsie.'

She went out on to the front step and surveyed them, her hands on her hips. She wished she were taller but at least on the steps she could look down on them.

'I'm sorry, gentlemen,' she said loudly, 'but Miss Fairbanks has gone. You've missed her, I'm afraid.'

'Gone?' They looked at each other blankly and then back at her. She felt suddenly powerful.

'Gone for a walk in Kensington Gardens. Oh, quite some while before you all arrived. Miss Fairbanks believes in healthy exercise first thing in the morning. She went that way.' She pointed helpfully. 'If you go up Exhibition Road, you'll find the Gardens over—'

But it seemed they knew the way. As one man, they clasped their notebooks tighter, folded their tripods and hoods, shoved their cameras into black cases and, lugging their cumbersome equipment with them, struggled off into the morning sun.

'I'm afraid I'm feeling rather unwell, Pootsie,' said Connie that afternoon. 'I have a headache. I fear you'll have to go home for the day.'

Miss Poots put her hand on Connie's forehead. 'Poor child. You do seem a little feverish. Too much excitement, or,' she added doubtfully, looking outside the window where the sun had vanished for the day, having put in a paltry appearance that morning, 'heat, perhaps?'

'It could be either,' mused Connie. 'It's come upon me suddenly. That's what happens with sunstroke, isn't it? We've had so little sunshine this summer I'm probably unused to it.'

'We shouldn't have taken a walk at Elevenses,' said Miss Poots mournfully. 'First Ida forgetting all about her lessons and gallivanting off with young Mr Thurston – when that girl has so much to catch up – and now you, Connie, dear, just as you were grasping the theory of pi!'

'I'm sure I'll feel much better tomorrow,' said Connie bravely, as she watched her governess gather up her handbag and bag of books.

Clasping her head, she led Miss Poots down the stairs. On opening the front door they found Arthur hovering at the top of the empty steps, looking sheepish. The journalists had not returned; they were probably still scouring Kensington Garden for Ida.

'Wrong day, young man,' said Miss Poots tartly.

Connie knew she was a little jealous of her closeness to the music teacher.

Arthur looked down apologetically; fibbing did not come to him easily. 'I left a songbook behind yesterday and I need it for another pupil. I'm so sorry to disturb you, Miss Carew.'

'Not at all, Mr Harker, please come in,' said Connie airily, and waved him into the hall behind her.

After she had shut the front door on her governess, who had recommended rest in a darkened room, she turned to Arthur.

'Wait here,' she ordered, and darted upstairs again.

Aunt Dorothea was safely out, seeing the solicitors. Connie went straight to the cupboard in her aunt's bedroom and on the top shelf, among the hat boxes where the box of newspaper clippings had been, found what she was looking for: a hat in black straw with a large brim and a veil that would hide half her face. It didn't go very well with her white summer dress, but elegance was her least concern.

She twisted her hair up and put the hat on, squinting into the looking-glass. She looked older and a little odd, but it was a most effective disguise.

Arthur had donned his black tie while she was

upstairs and appeared suitably funereal. He looked taken aback when he saw her.

'I say, Connie, you look like a mushroom. Is that hat really necessary?'

'Of course,' snapped Connie. 'I mustn't be recognised, whatever happens! She'll smell a rat. Now come on!'

They closed the front door quietly behind them and set off in the direction of Pelham Crescent.

The sky was overcast and the people passing them were dressed in overcoats and gripped their furled umbrellas as if, like Arthur, they didn't trust the summer. One or two looked curiously at Connie. She felt rather top-heavy, as if her head might wobble off.

'You remember what you've got to say, don't you, Arthur?' she said, clutching the hat and hurrying to keep up with his longer strides.

'I suppose so,' he said miserably. 'But I do hate all these lies.'

'They're in a good cause. We've got to find out the truth about Ida.'

'But if we're lying, we're as bad as she is.' He pondered. 'If she *is* lying, that is.'

'Not quite as bad. Hers would be a much bigger lie. Anyway, we'll soon find out if it is.'

The same maid Connie remembered from her previous visit opened the door to them. Fortunately she did not remember Connie.

'You're early for the session. That is,' she took in Arthur's black tie and Connie's mourning veil, 'I presume you've come for the séance.'

Connie pinched Arthur. He gulped and nodded. 'Yes, miss, we have.'

She sighed with irritation. 'No one else has arrived yet. We're not ready. Madam's not even down.'

'Have you somewhere we can wait?' enquired Connie.

For answer the maid ushered them into a small, cheerless parlour, its only furniture a circle of small uncomfortable-looking chairs. There were no pictures on the walls and the paint was spotted.

'You can sit here, I suppose,' she said sourly. 'I'll take you through when I've prepared the drawing-room.'

She shut the door on them and they heard her unlock the room next door.

Arthur sat bolt upright on his chair, his umbrella across his knees and his knees juddering. 'I'm not sure about this, Connie. Why don't we leave while we've got the chance?'

'Leave?' whispered Connie crossly. 'Buck up, Arthur. We can't leave now we've actually managed to get in!'

'It's all right for you. You're going to be an anthropologist. You're interested in people. I'm only interested in music.'

'And Ida,' Connie reminded him. 'Hum a tune then, if you're feeling wobbly.'

After several quietly mournful bars of 'Rule Britannia', the maid poked her head round the door.

'You can go through,' she said curtly. 'You'll be alone in there until the others come. It will put you in the right mood, I dare say.' She glanced again at Arthur's tie. 'I'm sorry for your loss,' she added, as an afterthought. 'May I tell Madam your circumstances?'

Arthur cleared his throat. 'My sister,' he said, in sepulchral tones.

The maid looked at Connie. Connie knew she didn't look old enough to pass off as Arthur's wife. She nodded sadly. 'Our little sister.'

This time the room was in darkness already, the heavy curtains drawn. Only the single candle burning in the centre of the round table gave out any light. It made it difficult to see anything when the maid had shut the door on them.

Connie and Arthur sat side by side at the table, waiting silently. Connie longed to leap up and draw back the curtains so she could inspect the cabinet but she did not dare. It was very frustrating. She pulled the hat further down her forehead; she seemed to have more veil in her mouth than on her face.

They had only been sitting in the darkness a couple of minutes when they heard the door knocker and then several voices in the hall, including Madame Vichani's; she had evidently come downstairs to greet her clients.

The walls were thin. They heard women's voices, perhaps two of them, and a man's, and then the knocker sounded again. There was the sound of Madame Vichani welcoming the latest client: another female voice. The words were indistinguishable but the timbre and tone were unmistakeable.

In the darkness Connie looked at Arthur, though it was doubtful he could see the horror on her face.

'It's Aunt Sylvie!'

There was only one thing Connie could do. She knew Aunt Sylvie would recognise her, even in Aunt Dorothea's hat. After all, her aunt had exceptionally sensitive powers: Connie respected that.

So, hissing at Arthur, 'It's up to you now!' she flipped up the baize cloth that covered the table and disappeared beneath it.

She couldn't see his expression in the dark but knew he would be looking aghast. For her part, she was very glad to take her hat off and most intrigued as to why her aunt was there.

It was even darker under the table, and dusty. She crawled into what she hoped was the middle, conscious that everyone's legs and feet would soon be coming down all around her. It was not a pleasant thought.

She gave Arthur's ankles a squeeze to reassure him and he let out a grunt of surprise. Then there was the sound of the door opening and everyone coming in.

Would Aunt Sylvie recognise Arthur? Connie didn't think so. They rarely met on Arthur's visits to Alfred Street West. And a séance was the last place she would expect to see her niece's music tutor.

There was a murmur above her; chairs were pulled

out and pushed in as people sat down: not as many as last time, perhaps six in all, including Arthur. Someone coughed, another cleared his throat, a lady gave a moan and was comforted by her friend.

Madame Vichani spoke, standing close to the table. As Connie huddled beneath it she could see the medium's jewelled slippers shining in the candlelight where the baize lifted. She drew up her knees, trying to make herself as small as possible.

'You are all here,' intoned Madame Vichani, 'because you have lost someone dear to you. Let me assure you that the veil between this life and the next is very thin. Few are able to lift it but I am one of them. In a moment I shall sit in my chair and channel your messages. The departed are as eager to speak to you as you are to them.'

There was the sound of a female sob. 'Will I be able to see my little Mary again?'

'They do not always show themselves,' said Madame Vichani. 'I will try to raise her. Is there any one else who has lost a small child?'

Connie thumped Arthur's foot. 'Er, yes,' he said gruffly. 'We – that is, *I* – have lost my younger sister.'

'I must warn you that if they show themselves they may look different.'

'In what way?' asked the woman.

'Time passes in the celestial place at a different rate. They may look older – taller.'

The séance started in much the same way as before, with the singing of a hymn. The mournful sound of 'Oh God, Our Help in Ages Past' trembled through the room.

Madame Vichani's contralto already sounded further away. Connie tried to peer beneath the baize, but saw only darkness. A murmuring began. She couldn't hear the messages that came for the group around the table above, only their amazed and often emotional reaction. The 'Captain' didn't seem to be present this afternoon.

Then light ringed the carpet around her. In the silence a girl's voice began to sing 'Baa, Baa, Black Sheep'.

Above Connie people drew in their breath. She could imagine how Arthur would be suffering, for the voice was decidedly out of tune.

'It's my little girl – Mary!' moaned her mother. 'It was one of her favourite nursery rhymes!' There was movement the other side of the table. A pair of feet shifted.

'Stay where you are,' commanded Madame

Vichani, her voice carrying to Connie. 'You cannot touch her.'

The light faded, amongst a hubbub of excited chatter from the clients.

'Silence!' Madame Vichani called out. 'You will frighten the spirits away. I need absolute quiet to commune.' There was a pause. 'Mary tells me she is happy. You are not to worry. She tells me she sings to you every night, though you do not hear.'

At this her mother burst into loud sobs.

'There, there, dear,' said Aunt Sylvie. 'We can't all have the gift.'

Madame Vichani was suddenly closer. Connie could see her slippers again, close enough to reach out and touch them. She was addressing Aunt Sylvie.

'And you, you have been here before and saw a manifestation also, did you not? Have you further questions for it?'

'Oh, no,' said Aunt Sylvie's voice. 'Absolutely not. The spirit has materialised, you see. It – or rather she – is living at home with us.' She added firmly, in case there was any doubt, 'As a living being, not a ghost.'

Exclamations of astonishment and disbelief went round the table.

'That is remarkable, indeed, if it is so,' said Madame

Vichani. Her voice sounded wary. 'So why are you here today?'

'I want to find out if a certain person is dead or alive.'

'May I know who this person is, in order to address her?'

'Her name is – or was – Sadie Turner. She was the child's nursemaid.'

15

Beneath the table Connie stifled a gasp. Aunt Sylvie was doing a spot of detecting herself!

Madame Vichani had drifted away again, presumably to resume her communication with the dead. There was the sound of curtains being drawn together and her voice floated across the room clearly.

'Sadie Turner? Are you there, Sadie Turner?'

A girl's voice, sulky. 'Yes, ma'am.'

Incredulous whispers above Connie, quickly hushed.

'And are you happy?'

'Yes, ma'am. They treat me a whole lot better up here. I get enough to eat, second helpings and all, and decent wages.'

'Thank you, Sadie Turner,' cut in Madame Vichani swiftly. 'You may return to your celestial plain.'

Again the jewelled slippers caught the candlelight. 'I think you have your answer,' said Madame Vichani to Aunt Sylvie. 'The young woman in question is enjoying herself in a better world, having departed this one.'

'Then that is most peculiar,' said Aunt Sylvie, 'since I am sure I saw Sadie Turner in our very street only this week. Of course,' her voice went dreamy, 'I do see ghosts from time to time. That is why I came here today. To establish exactly what I had seen.

'You see, I rather think she may have been involved in a murder. So if she were dead, she wouldn't have gone to a *celestial* plain at all, would she?'

A murder!

Connie, crouching beneath the table, lost her balance in her astonishment, toppled sideways and grabbed hold of Arthur's foot. But it wasn't Arthur's foot at all, she realised too late: it was far too dainty.

'There's a rat, a rat under the table!' screamed a female voice. 'It tried to bite me!'

At once everyone shot up, away from the table. Only one pair of feet remained: belonging to Arthur, who would be in a quandary about whether to desert Connie.

But there was nothing he could have done anyway. When Connie toppled over, her outstretched foot caught her hat and the next moment it had rolled out from under the table and, as Madame Vichani switched on the overhead light, there it was: a black straw hat with a damp veil, lying on the carpet for all to see.

'*Dorothea?*' Aunt Sylvie's voice sounded bemused. Perhaps she thought there was a tiny version of her sister lurking beneath the hat.

Everyone else except Arthur rushed out of the room, exclaiming about rats, manifestations and portents. Eventually Aunt Sylvie's feet followed them rather more slowly and then she, too, had gone.

'Come out!' said Madame Vichani furiously.

Connie crawled out and stood up. Her white dress was dusty and dishevelled, her hair was down around her face, but she looked the medium straight in the eye.

'Madame Vichani, I believe you are a fraud!'

Madame Vichani's eyes glittered. 'I remember you! The little troublemaker who wanted to poke her nose into everything. And you've brought another one with you!'

She turned to Arthur, who having stood up, decided

hastily to sit down again, as if it would make him less noticeable. 'You've not lost a younger sister at all!' cried Madame Vichani. 'You are here on false pretences! Both of you!'

'You use people's suffering,' said Connie. 'You make money out of them. You let them believe they can connect with their dead relations, their dead children. But it's all pretence, isn't it?'

'How dare you spy on me like this, you interfering girl!' snarled Madame Vichani. 'You and this youth here have broken into my house in order to accuse me! Of what, exactly? What do you know of the higher realms of being? You're only a child – ignorant, infantile and immature—'

'Now, look here.' Unexpectedly, Arthur rose and came and placed an arm around Connie. 'Connie is none of those things. She is going to be an anthropologist and a pretty famous one, I'll bet. Everything she does is for research purposes.'

Madame Vichani glared at him. 'Research, my foot! Another word for nosiness. You are trespassers in this house whatever reason you are here.' She drew herself up in her long black gown. 'I make people happy. They go away comforted. There is nothing wrong in that!'

'But you are lying to them,' said Connie. 'And your real name is Mrs Brown, isn't it?'

Madame Vichani's mouth opened in shock. In the harsh light she looked grey, the rouge standing out in blotches on her cheeks and the long golden wig garish against her skin. 'Are you accusing me of using a false name now?'

Connie stood her ground. 'I believe you are Mrs Brown and I think you take in girls from the Sisters of Hope Orphanage.'

'What if I do?' snapped Madame Vichani. 'I give them a position as a maid in this house. I pay them wages. I do it out of the kindness of my heart. They'd be on the streets otherwise.' She narrowed her eyes, her face hard. 'Wait a minute! Last time you were here you came with that other woman, the one who also came back today. You are in this together, all three of you. You want to denounce me and put me out of my profession! It's slander of the worst sort and I think the police will have something to say about it!'

She gestured to the maid, who had been standing silently at the door throughout. 'Fetch the key!'

'I have it here,' said the maid. 'I was about to lock up the room.'

Indeed, Connie could see a key in her hand, shining in the light.

'Then give it to me!' said Madame Vichani. 'We'll let these two dwell on their plight!'

'Come on, Connie,' said Arthur urgently. 'Time to leave!'

But it was already too late. With a slither of her skirts across the carpet, Madame Vichani had reached the door and shut it behind her. They heard the key turn in the lock.

16

Arthur sat down again and put his head in his hands. 'Now what?'

'Murder!' said Connie thoughtfully. 'That was what Aunt Sylvie said. That the nursemaid may have been involved in a murder. Perhaps it was Ida Fairbanks's murder!'

'I don't like all this research, Connie,' said Arthur querulously. 'It's getting far too dangerous. And now this! You realise it's going to get me into trouble with the Royal College of Music? I could be arrested!'

'Chin up!' said Connie. 'I bet Madame Vichani's only bluffing. The police aren't going to be interested. Séances are suspect anyway. The Law doesn't approve.' She looked around. The electric light overhead showed the room in all its threadbare shabbiness. 'This is a chance to investigate!'

'But we're locked in! How are we going to escape?

She could hold us prisoner here for goodness knows how long.' Arthur looked at his wristwatch and groaned. 'I'm meant to be teaching at five!'

They drew the curtains back, opened the shutters and tried the windows but they held fast, even with Arthur struggling to push them open. 'I think they're sealed,' he said desperately.

Connie began to prowl around the room. 'If the police do come, we need to prove to them that Madame Vichani is a fraud.'

'How do we do that? We don't even know if it's true.'

Connie bit her lip. She stared at the cabinet, which looked like an ordinary cupboard but with three sides. It was rather badly made, she saw in the daylight, of some cheap wood nailed crudely together, but surprisingly spacious, large enough to hold two people. The curtains were drawn back and inside was the chair that Madame Vichani used when she communicated with spirits.

She went over and sat in it herself, as if somehow the chair itself might possess paranormal properties and give her a clue to what was going on.

But of course it was an absolutely ordinary chair, straight-backed and with an uncomfortable seat.

The carpet did not extend as far as this corner of the room. As she looked down, she noticed something odd about the floorboards inside the cabinet. They had been cut away and there was a large square of wood, the same flimsy wood as the three sides of the cabinet, set into them and fitting clumsily. She tried to lever it up with her fingernails, but it wasn't possible.

'Arthur,' she called. 'Arthur, come here!'

Arthur came and looked at the square. 'That's rummy,' he said, scratching his head.

'It's a trapdoor, silly! I think it's the way the spirits come up!'

'How does she lever it up?' said Arthur. 'There's no handle.'

'They must push from below. Can we prise it open? We can escape that way!'

They looked at each other with the same thought. 'Your umbrella!' said Connie.

Arthur had hooked it over his chair at the start of the séance. He hurried over and fetched it.

'I hope it's strong enough,' Connie said.

'It's a good make,' said Arthur proudly. 'I bought that brolly in Piccadilly with my first wages. I was fed up with getting rained on.'

They inserted the point of the umbrella at the

worst-fitting edge and with a sudden clatter the trapdoor fell back like a lid and they saw a hole beneath.

Connie looked down. 'There's a ladder.'

'Hang on. We don't know where it goes.'

'It must be better than staying locked in here,' said Connie. 'It looks as if there's a passage down there. There's no one about.'

'Let me go first, then.' Arthur looked so determined to protect her that Connie allowed him to insert himself into the hole.

A few minutes later they both stood in the passage.

They were in a shabby basement beneath the upper floors of the house. The only daylight came from behind them, where stairs led up to the ground floor. In front of them was a closed door, presumably opening into the kitchen and the area steps beyond. There was utter silence except for the sudden rumble of an underground train beneath the house. When that had died away Connie looked at Arthur.

'Forward?' she whispered. 'There must be a back door through there.'

He nodded unhappily. 'Forward. And then run like Billy-o!'

'Wait for the next train then.'

They waited for the sound to muffle their footsteps. That was a mistake. If they had not waited, they might have heard someone come to the kitchen door and stand behind it. As it was, they crept along the passage as the train growled deep beneath them and turned the door handle as quietly as they could.

'Right,' said the maid. She stood, arms akimbo, blocking their way, and her face was grim. 'You think you've escaped, do you?'

Behind the maid Connie could see a kitchen, with the back door in the far wall tantalisingly close, and the area steps beyond the window.

Arthur clutched his umbrella tighter and blustered. 'Look here, you've no right to keep us here, you or your mistress. I call it a pretty poor show. Now let us pass!'

'Keep your voice down,' said the maid, 'if you don't want *her* to hear.' She planted her sturdy feet apart. 'I could call Madame Vichani,' she said. 'I could tell her I caught you running away.' She pursed her lips. 'Not that you could run very far. The back door's kept locked.'

Connie looked beseechingly at the maid. She had been watching her and noticed how she liked being in a position of power. She must have bullied in the past; now she was enjoying taunting them.

She made herself sound younger than she was. 'Please let us go. We meant no harm. I was interested to see how a séance worked, that's all. I'm interested in a lot of things.'

'Nosey, Madam called you,' said the maid, with a smirk.

'I know you can unlock the back door if you want,' said Connie.

'And how do you know that, miss?'

'There's a bulge in your apron pocket. It's where you keep all the household keys during the day, isn't it?'

The maid sniffed. 'I get into trouble if anything goes missing from the larder. We don't have a live-in cook, see, only a woman who comes daily. Madam is as mean as a ferret when it comes to food. I never get enough to eat. And as for wages! I'm doing two jobs, but only paid for one and a pittance at that.'

'Two jobs?' said Connie sympathetically. 'What's the other one, then?'

The maid jerked her head at the ladder. 'Up and

down that when there's a séance, and all dressed up in my special robe. One day I'm going to break my neck! 'Course the Captain does some of them, but I'm usually called for, too.'

'The Captain?' said Connie. She remembered him from her first visit.

The maid gave a hollow laugh. 'Knew him all too well back at the orphanage and never wanted to see him again! But when I arrived, here he was and here he's stayed.'

She frowned at Connie and went on in an aggrieved tone. 'Shouldn't have told you that. But Madam's so blooming stingy to work for and that's a fact. I thought I'd got lucky when she took me from the Sisters of Hope, but turned out I couldn't have been more wrong if I'd tried! A month later the other girl left and I had to take over the play-acting as well as my other duties. I've scarcely two pennies to rub together.'

'You poor thing,' said Connie. She paused and looked at Arthur meaningfully. 'I don't believe we paid for our places at the séance, did we?'

'What? Oh, no. Let me see what I've got in my pockets.'

'You'd better come through,' said the maid

grudgingly. 'Doesn't mean I'm going to let you out, though.'

Arthur emptied his coat pockets on to the kitchen table. A crumpled pound note and a sixpence. The maid scooped them up into her baggy apron. 'That'll just about make up for the trouble I'm going to be in on account of not noticing your escape!'

'It's enough for a decent music book,' said Arthur dolefully.

Then they heard the sound of Madame Vichani's voice, calling down the basement stairs.

'Is everything all right, Ethel? I thought I heard voices.'

Connie froze. Arthur clutched his umbrella tighter, his knuckles white. Together they looked imploringly at Ethel.

She grinned. 'Nothing to worry about, Madame V,' she called out cheerily. 'Just practising for the next séance, that's all.'

She tiptoed over to the back door and unlocked it, beckoning fiercely to Connie and Arthur.

'Now, scoot before she nabs you again!' she hissed, and they fled past her and up the area steps.

'I'm a pauper because of you, Connie,' grumbled Arthur, as they made their hasty exit from Pelham Crescent. He looked at his watch. 'At least I've still got time to make my five o'clock lesson, even if I have to walk there. I'll take you back first.'

'I can look after myself,' said Connie. She had a lot to think about.

He snorted. 'I don't trust you. You'll dream up one of your dangerous wheezes again if I leave you alone!'

Connie tucked her arm through his. 'Don't be in a wax, Arthur. I'll pay you back as soon as I can. Besides, we had to bribe that maid. It was the only way. We'd never have escaped otherwise. I could see she was sizing us up, seeing how much we were worth. Luckily for us she doesn't like her employer and wanted to get the better of her. Anyway, we've learned some important things.'

'We have?'

'I think that was where Ida was living before she came to us – she was taking part in Madame Vichani's séances! When I went with my aunts she pretended to be Ida Fairbanks.'

'Does that mean she isn't Ida Fairbanks at all?'

'I rather fear it does, Arthur.'

He stopped in the middle of the pavement. 'Do you know something, Connie? I don't care if she isn't Ida Fairbanks.' He drew himself up and thrust out his chin, looking surprisingly noble. 'I love her for herself. She's the sweetest, prettiest, most ripping girl I've ever met – and she sings like an angel. I'm not going to investigate her any more!'

'But don't you want to know the truth?' Connie asked, impressed by this declaration despite herself. 'The woman you love may be a criminal. And murder has been mentioned!'

'By your Aunt Sylvie, who, begging her pardon, is as mad as a hatter as everyone knows!'

'Not everyone,' said Connie. '*I* happen to believe that Aunt Sylvie isn't nearly as dotty as she seems.'

They turned into Alfred Place West and there, floating up the steps of the house in a lilac costume with matching hat and surrounded by reporters, was

Ida, escorted by Frank, who had his arm around her.

Arthur looked crestfallen. He eyed Frank's arm bitterly.

'I know it's beastly for you, Arthur,' whispered Connie. 'But you'll have her to yourself for a whole hour on Friday!'

'An hour! He's been taking her out every day this week! And anyway you'll be there.'

'I'll sit out of the way on the window seat and read a book, I promise.' She put her hand to her mouth. 'Oh, crikey! I've just remembered – Aunt Dorothea's hat! Whatever is she going to say?'

That evening, having ticked number 2, Connie added number 3 to her Plan of Action.

INVESTIGATE NURSEMAID

She put it in capitals because it was so important – indeed, she thought it might be the answer to everything. *Thank you, Aunt Sylvie!* she thought. The only trouble was she had no idea how to go about it.

During the next couple of weeks Ida was courted by Frank, in between her other engagements.

It seemed that, after all, she rather enjoyed going to dances and events. She was the toast of the season: her beauty combined with her decidedly different way of talking and down-to-earth manner was delightfully refreshing to the jaded society watchers. She met a bushy-bearded playwright called Mr Bernard Shaw, who was particularly struck by her accent; a Mr Conan Doyle, author of the Sherlock Holmes books, who wanted to know all about the mystery surrounding her reappearance, and a Polar explorer called Mr Scott, who wanted to recruit her as a member of his forthcoming expedition to the Antarctic.

Ida appeared to thrive on all the excitement, rising mid-morning for a couple of hours' tuition with the despairing Miss Poots.

'My ballroom dancing is coming along a treat,' Ida informed her gleefully. 'It's all the practice I'm getting. Don't need no lessons in that no more.'

'I wish I could say the same of your grammar,' said Miss Poots.

Another invitation had arrived to take its place among the array on the drawing-room mantelpiece – not to a dance, but to take tickets to a fund-raising garden party in Thurloe Square, the profits to go the "Angels" Charity. The Chair of the party committee was Lady Lamont, Lavender's mother, and Connie was most intrigued to see that the Angels' Charity supported three orphanages, one of which was the Sisters of Hope.

'Does the woman think we're made of money?' grumbled Mr Thurston. 'It's all right for her aristocratic friends!'

'I think we should go, Harold,' said Aunt Dorothea quietly. It seemed she had gained surprising courage and confidence from chaperoning Ida. 'After all, the Sisters of Hope was where Ida spent her childhood. We are so grateful for that, aren't we? And it's just before her birthday! We must take tickets for the whole family, make it a celebration.'

As the days passed, Connie observed everything that was going on, as she always did.

She sat silently at breakfast and noticed that Frank was becoming increasingly tense and his father more irritable. After bidding her good morning, with Frank's shining white smile now rather more strained, they more or less ignored her presence at the other end of the table, though they were careful to lower their voices.

Connie, however, had very sharp ears.

'I've given her cocktails at Claridge's, tea at the Ritz, supper at the Savoy and practically walked my feet off in the park! What else can I do, Pop?'

'Take her somewhere romantic at night, you stupid ass. And don't call me Pop!'

Masticating his breakfast, Mr Thurston flipped through the pile of envelopes beside his plate, his face growing redder and more ill-tempered.

Connie knew why.

The household was escaping Mr Thurston's control. His wife was gallivanting off to dances and a new life, her health magically restored; his son's advances to his stepdaughter had not yet achieved their goal; and there were bills and more bills to pay.

As Connie had already discovered, the bills that morning came from his hatter, yet another from his club, an ominous-looking one from HMS Revenue and one stamped Western Rockies Railroad Company, Inc.

The Rockies. They were in Canada, which had featured in the stories of Frank's travels. Was it the company he had worked for?

'But her social diary is full!' Frank was saying.

His father stopped demolishing his bacon and eggs and glowered. 'Her birthday comes up soon. You've got to do it before someone else does!'

It was high time to carry out her Action Plan Number 3, Connie thought.

The nursemaid. She had been looking after little Ida fifteen years ago. Now she could be anywhere in the vast, sprawling metropolis that was modern London. She could be living in one of the new suburbs or perhaps have emigrated to an outpost of the Empire. How would Connie find her?

Connie tackled the grown-up Ida first.

It was Thursday morning. Miss Poots had not yet arrived and Arthur wouldn't be coming until tomorrow. The day stretched before Connie, bleak and boring: it was definitely time to do some more research and she had about half an hour in which to carry it out before lessons.

Ida, still in her nightie, was lying with one leg thrust from beneath her flowered eiderdown, sleepily admiring her toenails which she had painted in Revlon's 'Pink Kiss'; Connie could see the red and white Revlon box on the bedside table.

'He's got a lovely voice and in a good light you could call him handsome,' she said dreamily.

'I should say so,' agreed Connie, 'and the accent is attractive. Where are you going today?'

'Oh, I don't know.' She sighed. 'Frank always tries to give me a jolly time. We've been to some very grand places. It's awfully sweet of him.'

Ida's vocabulary was now a slightly odd mixture of what she had arrived with and what she had since picked up from her posh society acquaintances and Connie herself.

'Listen, Ida,' Connie said in a confidential way, plonking herself down on the eiderdown. 'Do you remember anything about the day you went missing? About the nursemaid who was looking after you, for instance?'

Ida looked instantly suspicious. 'This is because you still don't believe me, ain't it? I can't tell you nothing more, so there! I was only two, Connie! I think it's perfectly hateful of you to question me like this!'

She lay back with a thump and pulled the eiderdown up to her chin, dislodging Connie, and glared over the top. 'Now leave me alone!'

'So you remember absolutely nothing?'

'That don't make me an imposter! Get out!'

A slipper hit the door behind Connie as she retreated swiftly.

The next person to try was Cook, who had been a kitchen-maid when Ida went missing. She must have known the nurse.

Cook folded her floury arms and looked carefully at Connie. 'I don't know why you're asking, Miss Constance, I'm sure. I hope you're not going to get yourself into trouble just when things seem all tickety-boo upstairs.'

'I'm curious about the day Ida went missing. She doesn't remember anything, of course. But you, Cook – do you remember the nanny?'

'Nanny Thurston? Oh, yes, though we didn't see much of her below stairs. She had her meals in the nursery. That's your Aunt Sylvie's room now.'

'What was Nanny Thurston like?'

'She seemed quiet, plain, nondescript. For all that, she was walking out with a young man at the time.'

'Do you remember anything else about her?'

'You're a caution, Miss Constance, you are! Quite the little detective! It won't do any good, you know, to rake it up again. It's all been gone over and over before. By the police, by detectives and by Mr Thurston. As for Nanny, she left, of course. I don't know where she went. She couldn't be blamed for what had happened, not really.'

'What had happened exactly?'

'You know as much as I do, miss. The little girl was snatched – kidnapped – but Nanny Thurston never saw who did the dreadful deed. The strangest thing was that whoever did it never asked for any money in return. It was altogether a rum do. Goodness knows what happened to the poor little mite and then she turns up here from an orphanage, fifteen years later!'

'Thank you, Cook.'

'Now wait a minute, Miss Constance! Why are you asking all these questions?'

Connie escaped upstairs. Aunt Dorothea next? She would remember the nanny better than anyone, but it didn't seem right to remind her aunt of that terrible time when she was so happy to think she had Ida back.

On the third-floor landing she paused. Ida's door was still firmly shut, Aunt Sylvie's partly open. Connie poked her head round the door.

Aunt Sylvie was sitting at her dressing-table, applying lipstick rather badly and peering at herself in the looking-glass; she was somewhat short-sighted. She had not yet put her wig on and the effect was rather like one of the hard-boiled eggs Connie used to decorate at Easter.

'Hello, dear,' she said warmly. 'Come in. I think there are things you wish to ask me.' Her eyes gleamed in anticipation.

Connie nodded, taken aback.

'You and I, we have so much in common,' said her aunt. 'We both watch, don't we? But we must be careful and you're so young to deal with it. This house is full of other eyes, watching us.'

'Who do they belong to?' said Connie, perching on a chair. She was used to indulging her aunt. 'Ghosts?'

Aunt Sylvie shook her head. 'The dead are less dangerous than the living.'

'Do you know something about a particular dead person?' said Connie cautiously. She saw her aunt's eyes dart towards her, bright, filled with light. 'I mean, someone who might have been *murdered*?'

'Murder. That's a dreadful word, isn't it?' whispered her aunt. 'I knew something was up, of course. That's why I followed her that afternoon.'

'Who?'

'The nanny. Sadie. I didn't trust her. Dorothea wasn't well when she employed her. A dreadful mistake.'

'So what did happen that afternoon?'

Her aunt's gaze rested on the looking-glass. She leaned forward, applied a little more lipstick and pouted her lips together. She considered her reflection, her head on one side.

'Time muddles memories, you know. I'm not sure I can remember exactly. But now we have Ida back with us we should all try to be happy, for Dorothea's sake.'

'If she truly is Ida,' said Connie.

Aunt Sylvie's gaze in the glass moved to her, shining with intelligence.

'I know, dear child. It's awfully hard. I hear that child crying in the night. I want to go to her, but know I mustn't. I'll hear things best left unsaid. So for Dorothea's sake, I remain in here and all around us the darkness gathers.' Her right hand fumbled for her wig and she squashed it on. 'I haven't had my breakfast tray yet. Could you tell Martha?'

Connie came out of the door and almost bumped into Frank.

'Hi there, Connie,' he said easily. 'Came up to tell you your governess is here.' He grinned down at her sympathetically. 'Time for lessons, I guess.'

'Thank you, Frank,' said Connie, and ran down the

stairs. She heard him knock on Ida's door. 'You dressed yet, sweetheart?'

Had Frank overheard any of her conversation with Aunt Sylvie through the partly open door?

18

For the next three days Connie pondered the next stage of her research and watched Ida.

Aunt Sylvie was right: there were other eyes watching Ida too.

Mr Thurston's and Frank's.

Both of them had a hungry look about them, as if they wanted to gobble up Ida and her inheritance. Frank was shouted at by his father when Ida complained of a headache and was unable to go out to lunch with him; Mr Thurston stayed out late at his club and the next morning at breakfast was in a worse temper than ever.

'I lost again,' Connie heard him snarl at Frank. 'One day my luck must change!'

'It had better be soon, Pop.'

'You're a right one to talk,' Mr Thurston hissed, one eye on Connie, who was looking at them through her eyelashes, though her head was bent towards her plate of kedgeree. 'We're desperate, boy. No bones about it. It's up to you now.'

Perhaps it was not the best moment for Aunt Dorothea to tackle him about installing the new electricity. She came in while they were finishing; Connie had been about to leave but she stayed in case her aunt needed protection from Mr Thurston's wrath.

'Harold,' Aunt Dorothea began, in a surprisingly firm tone. She was fully dressed, in a fashionable costume that Connie hadn't seen before. 'Harold, I really do think we should have better light in this house. Ida has a headache this morning and she had one yesterday too. She loves reading, you know – she's such a bookish girl, dear thing – and it's so dark at night. She'll ruin her eyes! And poor little Connie –' to her surprise Connie felt Aunt Dorothea's soft hand touch her shoulder '– has to carry a candle all the way up to bed with her on the fourth floor! It could cause a fire. I do think it's time we had electricity.'

Mr Thurston seemed to pop with rage. His eyes bulged. 'Electricity! And how on earth do you think we can afford to convert the house to electricity?'

'Oh, I don't know. Is it so awfully dear? I thought perhaps – while we were doing it we might replace the carpets, they're so worn, and some new paint . . .' Her voice trailed away as she took in her husband's expression.

Mr Thurston's fist slammed down on the table and all the plates and cups and saucers jumped together. As did Connie and Aunt Dorothea.

'You have simply no idea about our financial situation, have you?' he thundered.

'Isn't there enough money?' Her aunt sounded bewildered. 'But where's it all gone? Has your business failed, Harold? Have you been keeping things from me?'

'I can't discuss matters like this with you now, Dorothea,' Mr Thurston said, his voice suddenly icily calm. 'But please – never bring up electricity again. Or anything to do with the house. We cannot afford it. As it is, we must dismiss Martha.'

Connie looked up. Her aunt's face had gone white.

'Dismiss Martha? But she's been with us for years! She's such a loyal servant. Who will do the housework, help Cook?'

'There's the new under-maid,' said Mr Thurston impatiently. 'And Constance here can help out. She has plenty of spare time. We can't afford Martha's salary any more. It's settled. I'm giving her notice today.'

Aunt Dorothea hesitated. For a moment Connie thought she might argue. But she turned to go. When Connie caught up with her outside the door, she saw that her face was streaming with tears.

'Dear Aunt Dorothea, please don't be upset,' Connie whispered. She put an arm round her shoulders and they went silently upstairs to her aunt's bedroom.

Aunt Dorothea sat on the little sofa and Connie sat next to her.

'The thing is,' said her aunt, taking out a lace handkerchief and wiping her eyes fiercely, 'the thing is, I know he's been gambling. It's been like that since we were first married. Then he had the money to do it. But since then his business affairs must have gone downhill.'

She shook her head. 'He's never discussed it. I know nothing about his business, Connie, though I've asked. He's always said women shouldn't know about such things. But to decide to dismiss Martha without consulting me . . . !' Fresh tears welled in her eyes. 'And there's nothing I can do to stop him. He's in charge of our finances.' She put her head in her hands. 'As it is, I think he's run through most of my allowance. I gave it to him to manage, you see, when we were first married. I didn't know then – about his gambling habit.'

Connie sat quietly, holding her aunt close.

After a while her aunt said, with a final sniff, 'I shouldn't talk to you about this, Connie, but I always have, haven't I?'

'Yes,' said Connie, as she always did. 'You always have.'

'You're such a comfort. When you're my age, I hope things will be different for women, that they'll control their own purse-strings and won't be in such thrall to their husbands.'

'I'm never going to marry,' said Connie. 'I've got my career to think about, Aunt Dorothea.'

'So you have!' Her aunt laughed, a little wildly, as if she didn't quite believe that things might turn out differently for Connie. She must have forgotten that they were now living in a New Age.

'If Frank marries Ida, will it help?' asked Connie. 'Her inheritance will be kept in the family and I'm sure she'll give a share of it to us.'

Connie glanced up at her aunt and saw that although her tears had dried, her face was grave.

'Ida must marry where her heart takes her. Mine took me to my wonderful first husband, your uncle.

Meanwhile, whatever happens, we should be happy that Ida is with us again.'

Monday came. Amid more tears on all sides, Martha had gone. Even Aunt Sylvie emerged to bid her goodbye, saying darkly that it was a doomed day for all civilised society if it could not afford to keep its servants.

It was a grey afternoon, with rain threatening. Despite that, Mr Thurston and Frank had taken themselves off to play golf at Richmond and would stay out for supper. Ida declined to accompany them, despite the lure of being taught to play by Frank. Instead she took Aunt Dorothea to tea at Fortnum's to cheer her up.

She pointedly did not ask Connie to join them, though Miss Poots had gone for the day. Aunt Sylvie remained in her room, dreaming her dreams.

Connie wrote up her research notes. After a while, bored and lonely, she wandered downstairs. She thought she might chat to Cook before she, too, went home for the day.

But she never got as far as the basement stairs. As

she reached the hall, the knocker sounded on the front door and Connie hurried across to open it, thinking it must be her aunt and Ida back already.

But a stranger stood on the top step, a woman, neatly if shabbily dressed, with a drawn face beneath a cheap brown felt hat. She stared at Connie and seemed surprised.

'Begging your pardon, but who are you, miss?'

'My name is Constance Clementine Carew. Can I help you?'

'I'm looking for Mrs Thurston.'

'She's my aunt.' The woman must be one of her dressmakers, who sometimes came to the house. 'She's out at the moment but she'll be back soon.'

The woman hesitated. 'I can't wait about. Can you give her a message?'

Connie nodded and the woman took a shopping list from her handbag and tore a piece from it. She licked the end of a pencil stub and scribbled rapidly, leaning against the railings. 'Ask her to come to my lodgings. This is the address. I need to speak to her urgent.'

The address was a street off the Fulham Road. It meant nothing to Connie. She looked at the woman blankly, holding the scrap of paper. 'Can I tell her what it's about?'

The woman glanced around nervously and said in a low voice, 'It's about Ida Fairbanks.'

'Ida! What about her?'

The woman's face closed up immediately. 'I can't tell you that, miss. Tell Mrs Thurston to come as soon as possible.'

'But please – what's your name? Can you tell me that at least?'

'He left me years ago, but I'm still Mrs Crake,' said the woman. Her mouth twisted. 'Sarah Crake.'

19

Connie called after her, but Sarah Crake didn't stop. She hurried away with anxious steps, her head down, bundling her coat around her. She didn't look back.

Connie went back into the hall and sat down on a chair. She needed to think. So Leonard Crake had been married to that woman. What did she want to tell Aunt Dorothea so urgently?

Connie remembered Crake's hand squeezing her shoulder cruelly. If Aunt Dorothea went to see Sarah Crake, she, Connie, must go too. There might be danger – it could be a trap of some sort – and she couldn't let her aunt face such danger alone.

The minutes ticked by slowly; Connie watched them on the dining-room clock. Fifteen minutes passed. Half an hour. After an hour Aunt Dorothea had still not returned.

She and Ida must be having a jolly time together

in Fortnum's, thought Connie, and a pang went through her.

How was she going to tell Aunt Dorothea about Mrs Crake without Ida overhearing? Ida wasn't going out tonight. She would be with Aunt Dorothea all the time, and at dinner, too. And Mrs Crake had said that what she wanted to tell her about Ida was urgent. Perhaps Mrs Crake needed to tell her aunt tonight.

There was only one thing for it, Connie thought, after an hour and a quarter had ticked by in the silent house and she was becoming bored with waiting.

She would go herself.

She would convince Mrs Crake that telling her, Connie, whatever it was about Ida, was almost as good as telling her aunt – who, anyway, was not very strong and had never been to Fulham in her life and might get lost, whereas Connie herself had been as far as Russell Square – to the British Museum – more times than she could remember.

First of all she checked where the Fulham Road was, on the large framed print that hung in the hall. It was dated 1880, but surely things couldn't have changed so very much since then. She was relieved to see that the Fulham Road wasn't far away and passed through attractive-looking market gardens, coloured in green, and even ended at a Palace – though it was a very long road.

Next, money for the omnibus. She searched the various pockets in the coat cupboard and in Mr Thurston's dark overcoat pockets found some loose change: a penny, two threepenny bits, a sixpence and three farthings. It wasn't stealing, she assured herself: it was all in a good cause.

She put on her coat and hat and searched around for a pencil to write a note to Aunt Dorothea. It was pointless to tell Aunt Sylvie what she was doing: she would only forget to pass it on.

I am going out for a walk. I won't go far so don't worry. Hope you had an A1 time eating cake! C. C. Carew

Then she set off. It was only when she had at last caught the right omnibus, having asked various passers-by, and was safely trundling down the curve of the Brompton Road, that she realised she had left the piece of paper with the address on it behind.

She must have dropped it as she was putting on her

coat. It certainly wasn't in either of her pockets.

Luckily she could remember the address as if it was engraved on her heart. 5 St Maur Road, Fulham Road, SW. She repeated it to herself, then asked the conductor if he would tell her when they reached the nearest stop.

He looked at her curiously from under his bowler hat as he took her penny fare and punched a white ticket. 'All alone, miss?'

'I'm visiting someone.'

'Righto. I'll be back, miss.'

But he didn't come back. The horse-drawn omnibus rattled on and on along the Fulham Road, which was as long as it had looked on the map. There were endless rows of straight streets, with identical, narrow little houses, branching off from the road, mostly Victorian, but some more recently built; their porches and balconies looked flimsy, as if they had been made from Mr Thurston's matchsticks.

The Fulham Road wasn't what Connie had expected, though it was as long. Not a weed poked up between the pavement slabs, hardly a tree grew. London was gradually paving over the whole countryside, she thought. The market gardens had gone now, the little greens on the old map. Even the local town hall had new-looking extensions, in a cleaner stone, not yet soot-stained; with its elaborate carved decoration it looked too grand for such a drab area. The people looked respectable but drab as well, as they hurried along with drawn, washed-out faces.

She caught sight of the town hall clock and her heart sank.

Six o'clock. Aunt Dorothea would be back by now, in time to change for dinner. She hoped she wouldn't worry. Was this such a good idea, after all?

At last the conductor came back to her. 'Get off here, miss,' he said and pulled the cord for her.

Connie stepped down into the damp summer evening. She walked up the Fulham Road and turned left where the conductor had pointed. St Maur Road was unmade still, and muddy with the earlier drizzle. At least it was still light.

She crammed her hat down more firmly and looked about for number 5. It had a gate that needed oiling and a dusty front patch with two tired shrubs.

She went up to the front door and took hold of the knocker. She knocked twice and waited, holding her breath. Her heart had begun to thud.

It wasn't opened by Mrs Crake, but by another woman altogether. Her face was set in frown lines and she frowned now, at Connie. She wore a clean but limp-looking pinny and bedroom slippers, tied on with string.

'What do you want?' she asked, in a disagreeable tone.

'I'm looking for a Mrs Crake.'

The woman jerked her thumb over her shoulder. 'She's just back. You're in luck, if you can call it that.'

'I hope so,' said Connie.

The hall was so narrow it was more like a passage and smelled of cooking fat. She followed the general direction of the woman's thumb, to a closed door. The woman nodded briefly, shut the front door and slopped away up the staircase.

With the daylight shut out the house seemed even darker than Alfred Place West.

Connie knocked. She could hear someone inside the room, moving about, so after a minute she opened the door and stepped in.

The woman she now knew as Mrs Crake put her hand on her heart, ashen-faced.

'You gave me a fright, you did, bursting through like that! What are *you* doing here? I asked for Mrs Thurston. You're only a child!'

171

'I am very advanced for my age,' said Connie, as calmly as she could.

'You think this is a blooming lark?' demanded Mrs Crake. 'A jolly jape –' she mimicked an upper-class accent '– or something? This is deadly serious, girl. I wanted Mrs Thurston and I'm not saying nothing more!'

'I am sorry,' said Connie, with dignity, 'but my aunt was unable to come. You can tell me what is so urgent. I am most reliable, I promise you.'

There were two moth-eaten chairs in front of an empty grate. Connie sat down, without being invited. She was determined not to move before she had heard Mrs Crake's story.

Mrs Crake scowled at her, nonplussed.

A brown paper screen, torn in places, cut off half the room and through the holes Connie could see a lumpy bed and a table covered in an oilskin cloth, with a washing bowl on it next to the brown felt hat. A curtain at the window, one half of a missing pair, was looped back with tape to show a cramped back yard. The gas lights on either side of the fireplace weren't lit and the room was dank and gloomy, though spotlessly clean. It was filled with the sour chill of poverty; Connie had never been anywhere like it.

'Look,' she said gently. 'I need to know the truth about Ida as much as my aunt. After all, she is my first cousin. If you know something, Mrs Crake – something about your husband, perhaps – please tell me.'

The woman sat down with a thump on the other chair and set her mouth into a stubborn line. But she couldn't stop it trembling, Connie noticed. She was agitated and trying to hide it. Her eyes were large and glistened in her drawn face as she stared at Connie. She was trying to make up her mind, trying to decide whether to tell her.

Connie put her head in her hands. 'I've come all the way here to find you, Mrs Crake. Please don't send me away. You see, I think it's most unlikely my aunt will come. I'm the best audience you've got and I'm very good at listening.'

She looked up expectantly.

Mrs Crake dropped her gaze and shook her head, a hand pressed to her thin cheek. There were no ornaments on the mantel above the fireplace, no possessions of any sort to tell Connie what sort of a person Mrs Crake was.

But she knew already.

'You're Sadie Turner, aren't you?' she said softly.

'The nursemaid who was looking after Ida the day she disappeared?'

The woman drew in her breath. 'How do you know that?'

'Sadie is short for Sarah. My Aunt Sylvie has already seen you on a previous visit to Alfred Place West, when you'd lost the courage to knock. You knew where to come to find my aunt because you'd worked for her all those years ago. You had a young man at the time and he was called Leonard Crake and later you married him. You kept his secret for years and it was only when you saw in the newspapers that Ida Fairbanks had turned up again and is due to inherit very soon that you thought you should speak out and tell the truth.'

'It's not suitable for a young girl's ears,' said Mrs Crake, in a trembling voice. There was silence for a moment while Connie waited. Then she began to speak in a whisper, so that Connie had to strain her ears to hear.

'It will be a relief to tell it, I suppose. Or some of it, anyway.' The woman sighed. 'Yes, I was little Ida's nursemaid. Very young, impressionable. My first position, working in a big house, lots of other servants. It was a relief to see my young man on my afternoons off. Leonard Crake, he was called. I knew he wasn't respectable, but he was well off; I never asked where he got his money. He'd talked to me one day in the park when I was out with Ida. I didn't mix with the other nannies, who all considered themselves superior. I suppose I was flattered he fancied me. I wasn't good-looking, you see.'

Her hand plucked at her skirt. 'Somehow he knew the workings of the household even better than I did, the hours they kept, who they all were. Perhaps I told him too much. He used to meet me in the park and we'd sit on a bench while Ida slept or toddled around. We'd share tea out of a Thermos flask. I was terrified that one of the other nannies would tell and it would get back to the mistress, but it never did.'

She stopped.

'So then one day you met him in Kensington Gardens as usual, when you were out with Ida in the perambulator?' Connie prompted gently.

'It was a hot summer's day. Leonard and I drank our tea, though I would have preferred a cold drink. I must have fallen asleep, what with the sun and the heat. Ida was certainly asleep. When I woke up the perambulator was still there, but Ida and Leonard had gone.'

'Do you think Mr Crake kidnapped her?'

'Why should he do that? There was no reward offered afterwards. When he came back eventually he said he'd been looking for her. I was hysterical by then. I had to go back and face your aunt. I never mentioned Leonard. That was what I wanted to tell Mrs Thurston. I was loyal to Leonard, more fool me.'

'But afterwards you married him?'

'I couldn't get another position, even as a scullery-maid. Everyone knew me as the nurse who had lost her charge. It was all over the newspapers. I married Leonard because I thought he offered me financial security.' Her mouth twisted. 'And after a couple of years he left me. Now I do a bit of cleaning in these parts and scrape a living.'

Connie leaned forward. 'But you know something more, don't you, Mrs Crake?'

Her eyes widened. 'What are you talking about?'

'I'm talking about murder,' said Connie softly. 'You're suspicious of Mr Crake, aren't you?'

The woman who had been Sadie Turner ran her hand through her hair. She didn't look at Connie. There was a long pause, as if she were debating what to say.

'He'd done it before, I think – I can't be sure. For payment. I never should have got mixed up with him.

176

I'm not saying anything, but after Ida disappeared he was flush with cash.

'There's another thing. He tracked me down yesterday. I'd not seen him for years. He came in here and told me not to tell that he was there that day. He'd know if I did – he'd come back and do for me.' She bit her lip. 'I've got to move from here, miss, I'm that frightened.'

'You should tell the police.'

'You think they'd be interested?' She gave a hollow laugh. 'All over London wives are beaten up by their husbands.'

For once Connie did not know what to say. Eventually she managed, 'I am so sorry, Mrs Crake.'

The woman shook her head despairingly.

'I'll try to help if I can,' said Connie. 'I'll tell my aunt what you've told me.' She knew she would have to do so now: she could not keep this to herself.

She got up and Sadie Turner rose from her chair too. At the door she pressed Connie's hand. 'Take care, girl. He's violent. Warn the other girl too. And another thing –' she paused and her voice trembled '– while I was in Alfred Place my basement key went missing. I think he took it. He could get in any time.'

20

Connie let herself out of the front door as quietly as she could: she didn't want to meet the landlady again.

She slipped out of the front garden and began to walk quickly along the street, her heart beating hard. There was an unpleasant taste in her mouth; it felt dry and ashy. It was the taste of fear.

She wondered why Sadie Turner had not told her the whole truth. She had watched her closely and observed how often her eyes shifted away and she fiddled with the thin material of her skirt.

Only when Connie reached the Fulham Road did she stop and look about her.

The sky had darkened overhead; the evening was drawing in early after the rain earlier, and she felt lost and oddly disoriented in the grey wastes of Fulham, unsure for a dreadful moment which was the right way to go.

She asked a woman with a kind face which was the way to South Kensington and the woman looked at her blankly. 'South Kensington, miss? No idea. Never been there in me life.'

It must be to the right, surely? To the left the houses petered out and she could see a distant haze of green.

A horse-drawn cab pulled up as she was standing on the pavement, trying to collect herself. Out climbed a familiar figure. He paid the driver and the cab rolled away.

Connie's heart leaped.

'Frank!'

He stood smiling down at her, immaculate and elegant in his Homburg hat and three-piece tweeds, and absurdly handsome. For once he wasn't escorting Ida. She had him all to herself. And he would take her home.

'Gee, Connie. This is a surprise. What are you doing here?'

'I'm so glad to see you! I thought you were playing golf.'

'The grass was too wet. We gave up, Pop and I. Well, this is a coincidence, bumping into you like this! Time to get you back to Alfred Place, don't you think?'

She nodded uneasily and tried to smile. As they

walked along together, looking out for a cab, the pavement became busy with pedestrians and Connie saw in the distance the grand façade of the Town Hall.

'I must be interrupting your afternoon, Frank,' Connie said. She made her voice sound apologetic. 'What are you doing here, in Fulham?'

'Looking up an old acquaintance of my father's.'

Connie frowned. 'So you didn't see my note when you got back from golf?' she said carefully.

'I came straight here.'

'To Fulham? What was so urgent?'

'I told you. I wanted to introduce myself to this old friend,' he said easily. 'Tell her who I was. Chip off the old block, you know.' He smiled again, indulgent. 'Jeez, Connie, why all these questions?'

He had turned towards her and slowed his step. His tanned face looked too smooth suddenly, a mask that might hide the truth; his smile tarnished. Connie felt the revelations of Sadie Turner seep over her and stick like a stain. A chill went through her.

She gritted her teeth. 'I know you must have gone back to Alfred Place because you're not wearing golfing clothes.'

He held his hands up winningly. 'OK, I admit it, I did go back. I needed to change out of my things.

I saw your note and Pop sent me after you. We were worried.'

'So why did you lie?'

He shrugged irritably. 'What does it matter?'

'I didn't say in my note where I was going,' said Connie. 'How did you know to come here?'

He didn't answer, for at that moment an empty horse-drawn cab rattled towards them and he hailed it. 'Hey, that's good! We'll have you home in a trice.'

His hand reached out. Connie backed away, but he had gripped the sleeve of her coat.

'Where are you going to take me?' she said wildly.

His eyes narrowed. 'To Alfred Place, of course.'

Fear gripped her again. She looked at Frank's bland face with suspicion and saw for the first time that his bright eyes were too close together.

'Thank you, Frank, but I'd prefer to go home on my own.'

He laughed, showing his perfect teeth. 'Why, you think I'm going to abduct you or something, you silly little ass? Jeepers, wait a minute—'

Connie had wrenched away and was running through the crowds. She couldn't hope to outrun him, of course, not with his long legs, and it was too ridiculous running away from her step-cousin when all he wanted, probably, was to take her home. But he had lied to her. And how had he known she was coming to St Maur Road?

Frank was taken by surprise. He began by shouting after her, but she didn't stop. Then he had to cancel the cab, whose irate driver was waiting expectantly. Only then could he begin his pursuit of Connie in earnest.

It gave Connie a few seconds' start. She wove in and out of pedestrians. Being small was suddenly an advantage; perhaps he wouldn't be able to see her.

She dodged into a tobacconists' and bent low beneath the window, as if looking through the newspapers and magazines on display on the shelves.

She had been crouched double for some time when the tobacconist said politely, 'Can I 'elp you, miss?'

She picked up a bottle of lemonade and bought it for twopence, then surreptitiously left it in a corner when a couple of customers came in and diverted his attention. When she emerged there was no sign of Frank. She began to walk quickly, not running in case it would draw attention to herself, all the time desperately looking out for an omnibus.

She reached the Town Hall and was brought to a standstill by a crowd blocking her way.

Then she saw the reason: a group of suffragettes were gathered round the entrance, shouting 'Votes for Women' and waving placards. An official, red in the face, was shouting back: 'Go away! Disperse before I call the police!' People were watching with interest to see what would happen.

A woman in front of Connie turned away in disgust. 'They're everywhere, these bleedin' suffragettes! They'll start smashin' the winders next.'

'Don't you want the vote?' Connie asked.

'Bless the duck, what would I do with a vote? Not the same as bread and butter on your table, is it?'

'It might be,' said Connie.

Then she heard Lavender's voice rising with the rest but unmistakeable, with its cutglass vowels. 'Stop imprisoning us! No more force-feeding!'

She wriggled through, beneath people's arms. 'Lavender!'

Lavender turned towards her and beamed. 'Connie! Topping to see you! Where's Ida?'

'Eating cake. I thought your father had forbidden you—'

Lavender lowered her voice and winked. 'He doesn't know I'm here. He's away in Scotland at the moment, inspecting the estate. Have you come to support us?'

'Sort of,' said Connie. 'I mean I would if I had time, but it's not terribly convenient at the moment. Someone's chasing after me.'

'I say, how thrilling! Can I help? I've got the motor parked round the corner in Harwood Road.' She was, Connie noticed now, wearing a duster coat and there were goggles on a strap dangling round her neck.

'Yes, please,' said Connie. 'I'm trying to get away from my step-cousin.' She gasped as she saw Frank's head and shoulders above the crowd blocking his way; he was looking frustrated and furious. 'Oh, and I've just spotted him!'

'No time to waste, then!' said Lavender. She thrust her placard at another suffragette to hold and grabbed Connie's hand. 'Come on!'

She pulled Connie through the group of suffragettes and up the steps of the Town Hall, dodging the official who was still distractedly trying to disperse them.

'Where are we going?' cried Connie, once they were inside the lobby.

'We'll go out by the other entrance,' said Lavender, pushing through an elaborate panelled door into a hall with plastered walls and a beamed ceiling. 'The motor's parked very close to it.'

Connie trod uneasily over the mosaic floor, her feet leaving damp prints on the tiles. This place was like a palace and they were trespassers. 'But Lavender, what if we're stopped?'

'I'll just say who I am,' said Lavender carelessly. 'I'll say I've come to admire the new extension. They'll all be bowing and scraping, you'll see.'

And so they did, to Connie's amazement. First the porter from his box and then various gentlemen emerged from the grand rooms on either side and Lavender charmed them all, once she had introduced herself. A cultural trip for her little friend, she said, to show her one of the marvels of modern architecture. She hoped they didn't mind.

'Not at all, Lady Lavender,' they said, and bowing, showed them the way through the hall of the new extension with its green marble pillars, and out beneath a columned porch to the steps that led down into Harwood Road.

The motor vehicle, parked precariously half on and off the pavement, was surrounded by a group of small boys admiring its gleaming cream exterior. One urchin, greatly daring, had perched himself on the charcoal grey leather of the front seat.

'Shoo!' said Lavender, swatting him with her glove,

and he removed himself with alacrity. 'Grab a perch, Connie, and off we'll go!'

'You mean you drive it yourself?' said Connie, impressed, scrambling on to the back seat.

'Of course,' said Lavender carelessly. 'Baggott, our chauffeur, taught me.'

She rushed round to the back and cranked the starting handle. The engine made a frightening noise and died.

'Oh, botheration!' said Lavender. 'I've probably flooded it.'

'Here comes Frank!' cried Connie, in dismay.

She had been watching out of the back window. He must have realised they would come out through the other entrance of the Town Hall. Now he had rounded the corner and was surveying the street with a most unpleasant look on his face. He could hardly miss the beautiful shining dragon parked so close.

She crouched down and hoped he wouldn't see her beneath the canopy. 'Can you hurry?'

'I'm doing my best,' said Lavender irritably. 'I wish I could remember—'

But suddenly there was a splutter and a gasp and the engine roared into life. Lavender flung herself into the driving seat, clutched the steering wheel and put her foot down. The motor car lurched off the pavement.

'What ho!' she cried gaily, pulling her goggles up with one hand and snapping them over her eyes. 'Off we go!'

And so they did, in a series of hops and sprints. For good measure Lavender tooted the horn to the delight of the small boys, who raised a ragged cheer and scattered out of the way. But Connie, watching out of the back, saw Frank's attention, alerted by all the noise, focus on them. His furious eyes met Connie's and she gasped and shrank back.

'He's seen me!'

21

Lavender glanced in the mirror. 'If he was after me, Connie, I'd be jolly happy!'

'No you wouldn't. He's a beast! Him and his father.'

At that moment the engine stalled.

Frank was suddenly at the door. He put one hand on it and tried to wrench it open, while with the other he reached in and tried to grab Connie on the back seat. His teeth were bared in fury. He looked dangerous, altogether unrecognisable.

Connie brought her legs up and kicked out with all her strength. The heel of her button boot caught his knuckles and he fell back with a yell.

With a tremendous roar the engine started again. The motor gathered speed.

Not fast enough. Already Frank had recovered. He tore down after them in the middle of the road. He would catch up with them at any minute.

But the middle of the road is never a good place to run, even if it looks deserted. A rag-and-bone man and his trap came out of Tyrawley Road, the pony pulling the trap at a fast trot.

Lavender swerved violently, throwing Connie to one side on the slippery leather seat. Frank, in danger of flying hooves, staggered back seconds before being mown down. As it was, he was cursed by the driver, who threw a couple of filthy rags at him for good measure.

Meanwhile, the motor swooped safely round the corner and on to the King's Road, where they were soon in the thick of the traffic.

Connie clutched the strap as they careered along and tried to stop sliding about. She had never travelled so fast in her life. Her hair blew back and her eyes stung with the dust. It seemed to her that they were all taking part in a dizzying race – the horse-drawn carts and omnibuses, the cabs and private carriages, the motor vehicles – and most disconcertingly, there was traffic coming straight at them from the other direction and all the drivers on their side of the road seemed to be furious with the drivers on the other side, leaning out of their motor vehicles to shout something unintelligible but undoubtedly rude while they blared their horns. The neighing of frightened horses added to the din and the smell of manure and diesel was thick in her nostrils.

'This is jolly, isn't it?' shouted Lavender. 'Got the motor for my eighteenth birthday. I'm a natural at driving, Baggott says. Only took me a couple of days to learn.'

'Goodness,' Connie shouted back politely and suppressed a scream as they dodged a carriage and four.

By the time Lavender had negotiated the various streets back to South Kensington, Connie had decided that she too would ask for a motor car for her eighteenth birthday. It was a pity it was so far off. Travelling at this speed was definitely the most exhilarating thing she had ever done. And while she was away, being an anthropologist in countries where they probably didn't have roads, she could lend it to Arthur.

As they turned into the Brompton Road, she grew nervous. Soon they would reach Alfred Place West.

'I say, old thing,' Lavender said in a concerned way, as they wove dangerously around Thurloe Square. 'Something's up, isn't it? Want to tell your Auntie Lavender?'

Connie shook her head.

'Look, Connie,' said Lavender as they drew up with a clashing of brakes in front of the house, 'get on the blower if you're in trouble. Ida's got the telephone number.'

Connie bit her lip. She knew she couldn't do that: Ida would ask why she wanted it.

'Thank you, Lavender,' she said, 'You're a brick for rescuing me like this,' and climbed out. Then with a cheery wave from Lavender and another roar, her ally was gone.

Her heart sank as she looked up at the house. How was she going to face Frank? How could she explain to everyone else why she had run away from him like that?

Even as she hurried up the steps of the house, a cab drew up and Frank climbed out. She could see the dangerous glint in his eyes as she raised her hand to the knocker. But the door was opened almost at once, as if someone had been watching out for her from the drawing-room window. It was Aunt Dorothea, white-faced and tearful.

Although Connie hated to see her aunt so upset, quite a large part of her was guiltily glad that she cared. Sometimes, especially in the pre-Ida days, it had been hard to know.

'I am so sorry—' she began.

'My dear child, where have you been? I thought . . .' Her aunt pressed a handkerchief to her lips.

Connie put her arms round her. 'I need to speak to you,' she said urgently into her aunt's ear, as Frank stormed into the hall behind her. 'I'll explain everything.'

'I'm afraid your Uncle Harold is very angry,' Aunt Dorothea whispered back, as if she hadn't grasped the importance of what Connie had said. 'He insisted on starting dinner, even though you hadn't returned. And poor Frank – he hasn't taken Ida out for dinner yet because your uncle sent him to look for you. He must have searched quite all the streets in South Kensington!'

'In that case I wonder why he ended up in Fulham,' said Connie, loudly enough for Frank to hear.

To her surprise he didn't respond, but threw his hat on to the stand, as if he would rather be aiming a missile at her. He strode past them both, tight-lipped, and didn't look at Connie.

He went straight to the dining-room and opened the door. They heard him say, 'She's back.'

There was the exchange of angry voices. No doubt Frank was relating the whole sorry story, with Connie as the villain of the piece. A fist was slammed on the table, something smashed.

'Oh, dear,' said Aunt Dorothea in a low voice, twisting her handkerchief. 'I do so hate these scenes.'

Ida swanned down the stairs, dressed to go out and looking ravishing. She didn't seem at all put out at being delayed by Connie; instead, she beamed at her as if she had forgotten all about their previous quarrels.

'You little juggins,' she said affectionately, 'you should have come out to tea with us. That would have kept you out of trouble!' She looked at Aunt Dorothea. 'Did I hear Frank's voice?'

'Yes, dear, he's back.' There was a strange reluctance in her aunt's voice. 'I expect you'll want to go out for dinner now.'

'Rather, Mother! I'm starving.'

Her aunt still looked ridiculously pleased at being called 'Mother', Connie thought sadly. She took her aunt's hand and was trying gently to draw her towards the stairs so that they could talk quietly up in the safety of her aunt's bedroom, when Mr Thurston stormed out of the dining-room.

Connie had never seen him so angry before. His face was patched with red, his eyes bulged. There was grease around his mouth that he had not bothered to wipe away with a napkin. He looked altogether mad and she felt a tremor of fear.

'What have you got to say for yourself, young lady?' he spat at her. His breath smelled of cooked meat.

Connie held her aunt's hand tighter. 'Nothing. I'm sorry I've worried everyone.'

'Nothing?' roared Mr Thurston. 'No explanation for disappearing for hours?'

'No,' said Connie. 'I felt like a walk, that was all.'

For a moment she thought he would hit her and was frightened, though she tried not to show it. He was a massive man and loomed over her. Behind him Frank grinned maliciously.

'I'm sorry,' she managed to say again. Then Mr Thurston had grabbed hold of her shoulders and pulled her away, breaking her hold on Aunt Dorothea's hand and wrenching them apart. Connie's hat flew off and her head juddered as he shook her violently.

'Harold!' she heard her aunt cry out as she was flung this way and that. 'Harold! Please, don't! She's only a child!'

As the hall reeled about her, Connie was dizzily aware that someone else had entered the fray. Ida had hitched up her dinner dress around her knees and with a well-aimed kick of her high-heeled shoes got Mr Thurston's ankles.

194

'Let my little cousin go!' she cried. 'You're a great big bully, you are!'

He stopped shaking Connie and began to drag her to the stairs, his corset creaking ominously. Somewhere she heard her aunt sobbing, Ida yelling out. She was hardly aware of where she was going. Mr Thurston was half-lifting her up the staircase, panting foully in her face.

Then Frank joined him and took her other arm, and together they lugged her up and up. Connie, still too giddy to resist, opened her eyes and saw they were in the shadows at the top of the house, outside her room. The landing shook.

She felt Mr Thurston's great hand shove her towards her bedroom door. He was breathing heavily, his face suffused with purple. He looked a monster.

'You stay in there, do you hear?' he hissed.

'Gladly,' Connie croaked.

He took a step towards her and she retreated hastily over the threshold of her room.

'There'll be no supper for you tonight,' he thundered. 'If you were my daughter, I'd whip you!'

'But I'm not and I'm glad! I'd hate to have you as a father!'

For a long moment he glowered at her while she

gazed at him defiantly. Then his gaze fell.

'Gee, Cousin Connie, you do make things worse for yourself, don't you?' said Frank sorrowfully. 'Why didn't you come home with me in the first place? Now I'm afraid you'll have to go hungry. And we can't let you out. It's too big a risk. You might decide to go for a walk again.'

With a swift movement he took the key from the keyhole inside the door and slammed the door in her face, almost trapping her fingers. The landing shuddered again with the banging of the door, as if the whole house would topple. The key turned on the outside.

'There's no escape, Connie,' Frank sang out on the other side of the door. 'I've taken the key. I'll let you out when I feel like it and it may be some time!'

There were further tremors as the two men thudded down the stairs.

She tried the door. Useless. She was well and truly locked in.

22

Connie didn't mind about missing dinner – though she was, now she thought about it, rather ravenous – but she did mind losing her freedom. When would she be allowed out again? She knew Frank was right. There was no escape from her room, four storeys up at the top of the house.

She remembered she had heard that shortly after Alfred Place West was first built sixty years ago, four of the houses had fallen down. It was thought they had been run up too quickly in damp weather. It was damp now, with all the rain this summer. What if the top floor collapsed, taking her with it?

To prevent such foolish worries from creeping into her mind she took out her exercise book and looked at her Plan of Action. It gave her a good feeling to tick off 2. *Investigate nursemaid* but not so good to write down 3. *Investigate Leonard Crake*.

That was going to be dangerous. And she didn't have long to do it in. Ida's birthday was two days after the garden party and the garden party was tomorrow.

Dusk had fallen and though the street lamps had been lit outside, it was growing dark in her room, and soon too dark to read or write up her notebook without a candle. But not too dark to think.

Connie took off her boots, then sat on her bed and pulled the counterpane up around her.

Hateful Mr Thurston. Had he been angry because Connie had made Aunt Dorothea worried? He never usually cared about her feelings. It was much more likely to be something else, some reason to do with himself.

Frank had lied to her. Somehow he had realised she was going to visit Sadie Turner and would hear her story. He had wanted to get there first, but had failed. Harold Thurston knew this. *That* was what he was so angry about.

She had noticed something interesting about Mr Thurston's eyes. When she stared him out just now, he had looked for a moment not angry at all, but frightened. Why should Harold Thurston of all people be frightened?

And Ida – Ida who had so gallantly tried to come to

her rescue. According to Sadie Turner, she was in danger from Mr Crake. Connie knew this already, but she wouldn't know why until she had investigated him.

She sat on her bed, huddled in the counterpane, for a long time. She knew that three people – Mr Crabb at the Sisters of Hope; Ethel, Madame Vichani's maid; and now the nursemaid, Sadie Turner – had mentioned things that should help her solve the mystery of Ida Fairbanks, if only she could think hard enough.

The huge head on the wall looked at her, until the room grew so dark she couldn't make out its shape any more. It crossed her mind that it might detach itself from the wall and loom over her bed. But that wasn't thinking like an anthropologist, she told herself sternly. The real, human Mr Thurston was a far greater monster and so was Leonard Crake.

All the same, she went to the window and looked through the gaps in the balustrade beyond, down to the street, where the gas lamps showed that the view outside was as reassuringly familiar as usual.

A cab was pulled up outside the house, the horses munching at their nosebags. As she stood there, two figures moved across to it from the steps below and she heard the murmur of voices.

Frank and Ida.

Frank helped Ida up the steps of the cab and then climbed in himself, after a word to the driver. The driver flicked his whip and a few seconds later they drove off. She supposed they were going out to dinner, the dinner that she, Connie, had delayed, and then perhaps on to dance somewhere. How could Ida go out with him? Didn't she realise what a cad he was?

If only Mr Thurston would go out to his club as usual! Then perhaps Aunt Dorothea would let her out. But Frank had probably taken the key with him.

It was a long time since lunch. Her room was chilly and damp. She was hungry and cold. She wondered wistfully what they had had for dinner and whether to undress and climb into bed. Then she heard a soft knocking and a thread of light appeared under the door.

She ran to it. 'Aunt Dorothea!'

The key turned in the lock outside and the door opened.

It wasn't Aunt Dorothea; it was Aunt Sylvie, carrying a lighted gas lamp. She tiptoed over and set it down carefully on the bedside table. As the room bloomed with a misty yellow glow, she turned to Connie, a finger to her lips.

'Shut the door quickly, dear child.'

Her aunt plumped herself on the bed. She was

dressed in her flowing night clothes, a curious old-fashioned Victorian lace cap covering her bald head. She fished something out of the voluminous pockets of her wrap – cold mutton between two slices of bread and a piece of slightly slimy cheese – and offered them to Connie.

'Here, darling. I saved them for you from dinner. The best I could do, I'm afraid, but I thought you might be hungry.'

'I am!' said Connie gratefully and devoured them, while they sat together on the bed.

Aunt Sylvie looked at her, a triumphant glint in her eye. 'Outwitted them, didn't I?'

'How did you get the key from Frank?'

'I didn't.' She smiled. 'That key is mine. You see, years ago, when I first came to the house, this used to be my bedroom.' She looked around and shuddered. 'It was damp even then, spots on the walls. I didn't complain – I knew Dorothea needed me here and I was determined to stay. It had been a maid's room and next door was where the butler slept, so the maid was given a key for privacy.'

'Who slept in your room below when you were in here?'

'Ida's nanny, Sadie Turner. It was more convenient,

across from little Ida's bedroom and doubled as a nursery. But I kept the key to this room when I moved downstairs. They had to cut another one.'

'But why did you keep it?'

'I thought I might need it one day. And I was right, wasn't I?'

Connie nodded. 'How clever of you, Aunt Sylvie.'

Her aunt preened herself, pleased. Then she leaned closer to Connie and peered at her.

'I heard all the palaver. Such a noise. Are you all right, my dear?'

Connie wanted to cry, but she made herself say, 'Where's Mr Thurston now? He hasn't gone to his club, has he?'

Aunt Sylvie shook her head. 'He's waiting for Frank to come back. He's in his study.'

'And Aunt Dorothea?' Connie said hopefully. With Mr Thurston out of the way, her aunt might come and see her.

'Poor dear. She's so upset about what happened. She's retired to her room. She's taken a pill to help her sleep. She never stands up to that –' Aunt Sylvie bit her lip, as if she was going to say a much worse word '– husband of hers.'

'But she says he rescued her!'

Her aunt snorted. 'She can't think that still! He was after her money, that's all.'

Her snort turned into a chortle. 'Harold thought the Fairbanks fortune would go to Dorothea when Ida was presumed dead. But the trustees of the will persuaded the court that she was only missing and that they should hold it in trust in case she turned up before her eighteenth birthday. He must have been so put out!' She paused. 'My sister never wants to see the truth. She's always been frightened of him. Even when little Ida disappeared she didn't insist he offer a reward. Not that a reward would have brought Ida back.'

'You remember a lot about that time, don't you?' said Connie softly. 'Why did you mention murder to me?'

'Did I?' Her aunt looked surprised, then gathered herself. 'There was a murder that day.'

'Whose?'

'Little Ida's, of course. I heard them plotting it. That's why I was suspicious and followed her.'

'Who?'

'Sadie Turner,' said her aunt impatiently. 'I knew she was meeting her young man. He'd come to the house several times before and Cook had got rid of him. She didn't approve. So when Miss Turner set

203

off with Ida in the perambulator that day I followed her. I wanted to make sure she was looking after Ida properly.'

'What happened?'

'It was terribly hot. When we got to Kensington Gardens I sat down in the shade under a tree not far from the bench where Miss Turner and her young man sat. They didn't see me. Ida played about for a little with a hoop the young man had brought. It was too big for her and she began to cry. The young man picked her up and carried her off. That was the last I – anyone – saw of her. The young man never came back.'

'Are you sure?'

Aunt Sylvie nodded emphatically. 'I waited. I waited until Sadie Turner left herself.'

'Do you think the child was taken away and murdered?'

Her aunt leaned closer. 'I know she was.'

'How?' whispered Connie.

'I saw the money the day before it happened. I looked out of the drawing-room window and saw them together in the street. He was giving her a wad of notes. She looked terrified, such a little slip of a thing next to him.'

'Did you hear them plotting Ida's murder?'

Her aunt looked confused. 'I heard them in the house, I think. I watched and listened. I've always watched and nobody notices me. Even the ghost-girl doesn't notice me. They think I'm barmy, not of any consequence.'

'The ghost-girl? You mean Ida? She's not a ghost, Aunt, I've told you before.'

'Of course. Sometimes I forget . . . Well, she's not Ida Fairbanks, anyway,' Aunt Sylvie added tartly. 'She can't be. Ida's murdered.' She leaned closer to Connie and whispered, 'Can a ghost be murdered twice, do you think?'

'Listen, Aunt Sylvie,' Connie said, trying to pull herself together. 'Have you told anyone else about this? Did you tell the police at the time?'

Her aunt opened her eyes wide. 'Oh, no, dear. Everyone thinks I'm loopy, I told you. But you don't. That's why I'm telling you now.'

'Don't tell anyone else,' Connie whispered urgently. 'Keep it to yourself. There's a dangerous man—'

'Sadie's young man? I recognised him the other day. He's come back, hasn't he?' Aunt Sylvie stared earnestly into Connie's face. The gaslight made hollows in her soft, round cheeks. 'But it's you who must be careful, not me, now you know my secret.'

23

After Aunt Sylvie had padded out of the room, Connie waited for a few minutes, listening at the open door.

Her aunt had taken the gas lamp with her, but light reflected up from the landing beneath. She heard her aunt's door shut. In her stockinged feet she tiptoed on to the landing and listened again.

The whole house seemed to be listening too, but there was nothing to hear except the springs protesting as Aunt Sylvie climbed into bed and her sigh as she reached for her cold Ovaltine. Mr Thurston's study on the ground floor was too far away for Connie to hear his customary grumbles and grunts, the creak of his corset as he leaned over his desk, the slamming of his fist as he glared at his correspondence.

It was the ideal time for Connie to tell Aunt Dorothea about her visit to Sadie Turner.

She locked her bedroom door behind her with

Aunt Sylvie's key, so as to fool anyone who checked. She took the key with her and edged down the stairs in the half-darkness, avoiding the holes in the carpet. The gaslight on the landing below glowed up on her cautious feet.

Two landings to go. If she couldn't hear Mr Thurston, did it mean he couldn't hear her? She had a horrible feeling he was lying in wait and might suddenly pounce on her out of the shadows.

Past Aunt Sylvie's landing and safely on to the next flight of stairs that would take her down to Aunt Dorothea's bedroom. That negotiated, Connie hovered outside and then, very quietly, turned the handle.

She stood in the doorway. The room inside was in darkness, the shutters closed. She could just make out the darker shape of the bed. She opened the door a little wider to let in more light from the landing.

'Aunt Dorothea! Wake up! Please wake up!' she hissed, not daring to raise her voice.

Nothing happened. Her aunt didn't stir. Whatever she had taken to make her sleep had certainly done so. Connie could hear her breathing, deep and regular.

She hovered, undecided. She didn't want to force her aunt awake, yet there was so much she should tell her.

As she hesitated, the front door opened two floors down. Ida and Frank had come back. Mr Thurston's study door burst open, as if he had been waiting for their return all evening.

Connie didn't linger. She shut Aunt Dorothea's door and tiptoed swiftly back up the stairs, as voices were raised far below in the hall. It came to her, as she darted upwards, that if she couldn't speak to Aunt Dorothea tonight, she must at least warn Ida. And Ida must tell her the truth.

Ida's bedroom door was partly open, the gas burning low, illuminating the usual scatter of clothes and toiletries.

Connie could hear Ida running up the stairs. She was about to slip into the room when she realised someone else was running up too, chasing behind Ida – someone with a heavier tread.

Frank? Or Mr Thurston?

Connie left the landing and climbed swiftly up into the darkness above. She perched on the top stair, straining her ears, ready to run.

They had reached Ida's landing below her. It was Frank in pursuit! From where Connie was sitting she couldn't see them but she could hear.

There seemed to be a scuffle. Ida's voice was

outraged. 'Let go of me!'

Frank's voice, desperate, pleading. 'Ida, I beg you! We've had a good time, haven't we? We're two of a kind. We make a good couple.'

'I'm sorry, Frank. I didn't realise—'

'Is there someone at one of the dances you've been going to?'

'No!'

'There must be someone else!'

'I wish there was.' Ida's tone was wistful.

'Well, then, marry me!'

'I can't and that's a fact, Frank. So don't keep on about it.'

There was a flash of pale green silk as Ida dodged away from him, into the landing's gaslight.

'But I know what you are, Ida!'

Ida turned, her fair hair shining in the light. 'What do you mean?' she said uncertainly.

'You're a fraud – a scheming little minx, aren't you?'

'I don't know what you're talking about.'

'Oh, come on, Ida. I've known all along.' Frank's tone became wheedling. 'If you marry me, I'll never tell. It will be our secret.'

There was a pause. Frank's voice softened. Connie

imagined his charming, rueful grin, his hands spread, his handsome head on one side. 'You see,' he said earnestly, 'I've fallen in love with you, Ida, whoever you are.'

Ida moved out of the light as she confronted him.

'Tosh! I think you've been out to catch me ever since you arrived. Courting me with your soft words and your jaunts to flash places. Well, it don't wash with me! I should have known we wasn't just having fun.'

'Gee, Ida,' Frank said angrily. 'You play a dangerous game! Impersonation carries a long prison sentence. Do you want that? Languishing in a prison where the other women are violent and out to harm you in order to survive themselves? And you've lied since the beginning, haven't you?'

Ida remained defiant but she sounded shaken. 'Prove it!'

'Oh, I will. Think how upset my stepmother is going to be when she finds out! But meanwhile you'd better watch out.'

In the darkness above Connie held her breath. She heard Ida retort, 'Are you blooming threatening me?'

'Just one little word, Ida, is all it takes. Say yes, you'll marry me.'

On the landing below there was a long silence.

'Come on, Ida,' Frank said, his voice gentle again. 'If you marry me, we can forget what you've done. No one need ever know.'

At last Ida said, 'I'll think about it, Frank. That's the best I can do.'

'That's my girl.' Frank sounded triumphant. 'You'll come round in the end, I know it. You'll see sense. After all, there isn't a choice, is there?'

Connie waited until Frank had gone downstairs. Then she crept down and went noiselessly to Ida's door. It was closed. From inside came the sound of sobbing.

As she stood wondering whether to go in, Aunt Sylvie emerged from her room opposite. She looked aggrieved.

'What was going on? Such a noise!' she hissed.

'A lovers' tiff, that's all. Nothing to worry about, Aunt Sylvie.'

Her aunt pointed indignantly at Ida's door. 'She's crying again. It wakes me every night. Can't you tell her to stop?'

'I don't think so,' whispered Connie. 'She's got a lot to cry about.'

Her aunt glanced at her sharply. She looked remarkably wide-awake for someone whose sleep had just been disturbed. 'You'll work it out, won't you, dear? For all our sakes? There isn't long.'

'Long until what?'

'Why, until Ida's eighteenth birthday, of course.'

24

Bessie, who had been swiftly promoted from under-maid to Martha's replacement, brought Connie's breakfast up on a tray. Out of habit she knocked at the bedroom door – which Connie had carefully locked again – then unlocked it and entered somewhat breathlessly.

'Oh, them stairs!' she said, just as Martha used to do.

Connie looked gratefully at her bowl of Post Toasties. 'Thanks, Bessie.'

'There – you're free now, miss!'

Bessie was garrulous and self-important now that she was under-maid no longer and slept next door instead of in the basement. She surveyed Connie, hands on hips.

'Ooh, you've been in hot water, haven't you, miss? But Madam – she made Mister Frank give the key over to me this morning. Said did he expect you to do lessons with Miss Poots on an empty stummick? I heard it all in the morning-room when I was serving.'

'Did you hear anything else?'

'They was discussing whether you was allowed to go to the charity garden party today. Madam said yes, the Master no.'

'So who won?'

Bessie looked at her without sympathy. 'The Master, I'm afraid, Miss Constance. And I'm to take the key away with me, not to leave it hanging about in your door. He doesn't want you going and that's flat, he says. It's part of your punishment. He's going to lock you in again, I do believe, while they all go off.'

After she had left, Connie poured milk on her Post Toasties and began to crunch them.

'But I will be going,' she whispered, and she felt under her pillow with her left hand and touched Aunt Sylvie's key. After what Aunt Sylvie had told her the night before she knew she had to attend that garden party whatever happened. Apart from those going from her own house, she was sure that there would also be certain key figures from the Sisters of Hope. She couldn't leave Ida unguarded and at the mercy of her would-be murderer.

'It's up to you, Connie Carew!' she said to herself.

That morning, Ida, still red-eyed from the night before but somehow even more beautiful in her grief, let out a sob when she couldn't remember her twelve times table.

Miss Poots, in some distress, for she had clearly grown fond of her unusual pupil, patted her on the back. 'There, there, dear. It doesn't come easily to us all.'

'Think of money,' suggested Connie. 'We always need that. Twelve pence in a shilling, twenty shillings in a pound.'

'But it's money that's the problem!' cried Ida and began to cry in earnest. 'He's got none, you see. I've always known that.'

'Ah, Love,' said Miss Poots, pursing her lips in disapproval. 'Is that what it's all about?'

'Yes,' admitted Ida dolefully. 'I wish . . .'

Connie touched Ida's arm. 'Don't worry. He's not worth it.'

Ida sniffed. 'Isn't he?'

'He's a rotter, Ida. He wants your inheritance, that's all. You can't love him!'

'Oh,' said Ida, looking perplexed. 'But I think I do, you see.'

Miss Poots looked plaintively at them both. 'May we please get back to the logical world of maths?'

By the time of Arthur's music lesson Ida had miraculously cheered up.

Connie, perched on the window seat in the sunshine, tried to hear what was going on. She wondered if two proposals in twenty-four hours might be a bit much for Ida.

She glanced over. Nothing seemed to be happening over at the pianoforte. Arthur was bent over Ida as she tried to play Chopsticks, running his hands through his hair in an agitated way. Things went better when she began to sing 'Cherry Ripe'. He beamed, as her pure soprano soared through the room.

'We'll try some operetta next time,' he said. 'I only wish you could accompany me this afternoon.'

Ida looked at the floor. 'So do I. Where are you going?'

'A charity garden party in Thurloe Square, given by Lady Lamont. I'm to play the piano. She's getting the one from her drawing-room carted across somehow.'

At that Connie leaped up from the window seat.

216

'We're going too! That is, Ida's going. I'm to be locked up.'

She tried to signal with her eyes that despite that, she intended to escape, but he did not appear to understand. He was gazing at Ida, looking positively elated and not at all upset by Connie's cruel incarceration.

She tried to have a word with him alone at the front door as he was leaving, but to her annoyance Ida was suddenly there behind her.

'So I'll see you later, Arthur?' Ida said.

'He's just said so,' said Connie impatiently.

'Arthur?'

Arthur stood on the top step and looked at Ida, then at Connie. Some emotion seemed to get the better of him: he went bright pink and was rendered speechless. In the end he stumbled down the steps without saying goodbye to either of them.

Ida slapped her music book against her skirt and went into luncheon, her head bent.

Connie knew Arthur had wanted to say something to her about the garden party, but couldn't because of Ida being there. Frowning, she followed Ida into the dining-room.

Everyone was in there, except for Mr Thurston, who was lunching at his club as usual.

217

Connie noticed that Ida did not look at Frank. Neither did she. Aunt Sylvie smiled vaguely around the table at nobody in particular. Aunt Dorothea was largely silent and picked at her food, while Frank cracked jokes that made no one laugh except Miss Poots, with her high tinkle.

It was altogether a most uncomfortable lunch.

When Frank had excused himself and left, Aunt Dorothea leaned across to Connie.

'Connie, dear, I'm sorry about the garden party, but Uncle Harold thinks you shouldn't be allowed a treat so soon after yesterday. You did give us all a dreadful fright, you know.'

'Did I? I'm so sorry, Aunt Dorothea.'

'I know you are. But Uncle Harold says you must remain locked in your room. He doesn't trust you. I do, of course, but I can't change his mind.'

'Could I talk to you, Aunt Dorothea? I need to explain things.'

'Of course. Why don't you come to my room after lessons while Bessie and I are sorting out my clothes for the garden party?'

'Privately, I mean.'

'Then tonight, when I get back. There'll be plenty of time then. You'd better run along to lessons now.'

'But—'

'Come along, Connie,' said Miss Poots, rising from the table. 'I don't want to lose both my pupils this afternoon.'

She looked meaningfully at the empty seat recently occupied by Ida, who had already disappeared to prepare herself for the party.

Not that Ida *can* make herself more beautiful, Connie thought sourly, as she trudged off behind Miss Poots.

By the time lessons had ended and Miss Poots had gone, Mr Thurston had returned. The whole household gathered in the hall in their finery.

Connie in her everyday pinafore and black stockings stood on the stairs watching them. She noticed how stiffly Aunt Dorothea put her arm through Mr Thurston's and did not meet his gaze, and how awkward Ida was with Frank when he offered her his arm.

As if suddenly remembering Connie, Mr Thurston turned to Frank. 'Get that child locked up!' he barked.

Frank abandoned Ida, took the stairs two at a time and advanced on Connie with a rueful grin. 'Gee, I'm sorry for this, cousin.'

'No, you're not! And, incidentally, you're no cousin of mine!'

Frank's smile faded. He shrugged. 'OK. Are you going to go quietly or do I have to carry you?'

'I'll go quietly,' said Connie, with dignity.

In her bedroom she heard him turn the key in the lock outside. She smiled to herself.

She waited. His feet pounded away down the stairs.

Sound travelled up through the floorboards of the house. She heard them leave the hall, the slam of the front door, and when she raised the window she heard them go down the steps to the sunlit street outside. Such a short walk to Thurloe Square: she mustn't waste any time.

Quickly she threw off her clothes and pulled on a blue muslin dress and white stockings. There was a soft white muslin hat in her wardrobe: that would do splendidly for a garden party.

She crammed it on her head and then went over to her bed.

She slid her hand under the pillow. Her fingers searched and found nothing, only the smoothness of the sheet beneath. In desperation she lifted the pillow and looked.

The key had disappeared.

Of course! Bessie had made the bed that morning. Why hadn't she thought of that? The traitor Bessie, who had been making sheep's eyes at good-looking Frank since she first arrived. She must have passed it to Frank, so now he possessed both keys.

Connie sank down on her bed. What was she to do?

She didn't think for long. There was only one thing she could do. It was risky, it was daring, it was dangerous and she'd never attempted it before. But she knew she had to do it.

25

She found an empty hatbox on the top shelf of the wardrobe and squashed the hat in. She would have to take it with her, which was a great nuisance, but one couldn't go hatless to a garden party.

When she pushed up the window the hatbox just fitted through and landed with a thud on the smooth grey tiles the other side. She wasn't strong enough to push the window up very far, but she was agile and not much wider than the hatbox. She could wriggle through without much difficulty if she held her breath.

She stood up uncertainly on the tiles the other side. The street seemed dizzily far below and she ducked down hastily. The balustrade was some protection so, pulling the hatbox with her by its carrying string, she began to crawl along, as close to the house wall as possible, trying to avoid the gutter by the balustrade where water had puddled after the rain.

It wasn't far to the neighbouring house. Of course the twins Cecil and Claud might be out with their nanny in Kensington Gardens but they would probably be back in the nursery now. She hoped they would be alone.

She looked through the window. Inside, the two little boys, dressed in miniature sailor suits, were playing with their railway track. There didn't seem to be a grown-up with them, though she couldn't see right into the room. She knocked softly on the glass and they both gazed up with identical expressions of horror.

'Open it,' she mouthed, knowing they wouldn't be able to hear. 'Please open it!' She made desperate signs at the window, but they looked more terrified still.

'It's me!' she cried. 'Don't you remember me? I came to tea once.'

They couldn't hear her. She knocked again and they drew close together, their small faces pale. Connie stared at them in exasperation. What silly babies they were!

Then someone strode across the nursery floor behind them.

The window was pushed up. A boy of about Connie's age poked his head out. He didn't look either particularly friendly or unfriendly and certainly not in the least scared: he looked as if girls knocked on the wrong side of the nursery window every day.

'Hello.'

'Hello,' said Connie. 'Who are you?'

'Surely who *you* are is more to the point,' he said loftily. 'Are you a burglar?' He flicked a dismissive thumb in the direction of the twins. 'If so, there's nothing they own that's worth stealing.'

'I know. I've been to tea. Could you let me in, please? I need to escape through your front door.'

His lordly expression vanished. 'Escape? I say, how ripping! You'd better come in at once, then. Have you been a prisoner?'

Connie climbed in with the hatbox and smoothed herself down. Her blue dress was sadly dirty and damp about the knees. 'Yes,' she said curtly, 'and I need to get to Thurloe Square urgently.'

The boy thrust out his hand. 'Robert Cavendish. I'm the twins' cousin, worse luck.'

Connie put her hand out too. 'Constance Clementine Carew. I live next door.'

The twins gazed at Connie wide-eyed and plugged their pink thumbs into their mouths.

Robert stuck his head beneath the open window

and gazed thoughtfully at the tiled passageway between the houses. When he withdrew it Connie thought he looked at her with a new respect.

'We're going to have to be awfully quick,' he said. 'The nanny is downstairs, getting their grub, but she won't be long.'

'What about their parents?'

'They're in their rooms, dressing for some garden party.'

He opened the nursery door, listened and beckoned silently to Connie. She sped after him.

She had followed him down the top flight of stairs when she realised that Cecil and Claud were trailing after them. She nudged Robert and pointed back up.

'Go away,' he hissed at the twins. 'You'll ruin everything!' He quickened his pace down the stairs, but two flights down they were still following like limpets.

Connie couldn't help noticing how luxurious this house was compared with her own: thick carpets, glossy paint, a shining bannister rail. It smelled of fresh flowers and furniture polish. The electric lights overhead were on, even on this sunny summer's day.

As they reached the third-floor landing, a bedroom door opened and out came a woman who Connie realised must be Mrs Cavendish. She looked at Connie, hot and breathless behind Robert, and raised her immaculate eyebrows, as if she knew immediately that Connie was a usurper in their perfect house.

'And who is this?'

There was a pause. Connie's mouth dried.

Then from somewhere behind her the voice of Cecil – or possibly Claud – piped up, 'It's Connie Carew, from next door, Mama. She came to tea with us and Nanny.'

Mrs Cavendish's powdered face cracked into a cautious smile. 'So nice to meet you, my dear.' A bony hand, heavy with rings, was offered and Connie took it gingerly in her grubby one.

'I'm just showing her out, Aunt,' said Robert.

'Good boy,' said Mrs Cavendish in a relieved way, and vanished back into her bedroom, dusting her hand.

'Thanks for rescuing me,' said Connie, as Robert opened the front door. Behind him the twins murmured something unintelligible, nodding wisely at each other.

'Bunk off, you two,' said Robert. He shuffled his feet on the doorstep. 'Glad to help. If you must know, it's beastly boring staying here. My people make a silly fuss if I want to do anything.'

'Same with me,' said Connie sympathetically.

'Perhaps I'll see you again.'

'Perhaps,' said Connie. She opened the hat box, took out the white muslin hat and pulled it well down over her eyes. 'I wish this was a better disguise,' she muttered to herself.

'Are you still escaping?' asked Robert.

'There isn't time to explain properly, but I think someone's going to murder my cousin.'

Robert stared at Connie with a thrilled expression. She thrust the empty hat box at him and left him standing on the steps, gazing after her and dangling it from one hand.

26

Thurloe Square was clogged with carriages and motor vehicles. Connie threaded her way between them and walked all the way round the iron railings of the garden, noting that the three gates – the broadest on the south side and two others, west and east – were open. This might be useful information for later.

The guests were parading through from all directions, languid ladies in broad-brimmed hats, abundantly strewn with artificial flowers, cherries and stuffed birds; suave gentlemen in top hats and frock coats. A few were accompanied by children, no one younger than Connie.

She attached herself to one party: a husband and wife with a sulky-looking daughter, also dressed in blue muslin, and managed to slip in with them through the south gate.

The girl noticed Connie dogging her footsteps and

glared, but beneath the brim of her enormous hat her mother wasn't capable of noticing anything unless it was immediately in front of her, while her husband was occupied in handing over their tickets. There were a couple of policemen standing back and watching the guests as they came in through the gate, but they must have thought Connie was a member of the family.

As soon as she was inside, she darted away up a gravel path that looked deserted. She hid in the heavy shade of the trees that edged the garden and peered through a tangle of greenery to the sunlit lawns beyond. She had never been in the garden of Thurloe Square before and needed to study its lay-out.

In the middle was a small but imposing mound, surrounded by a bed of rhododendrons. A path ran round this in a diamond shape and from it other paths branched away into a main one that bordered what was really a rectangle, not a square at all. Years before, the gardens must have been planted with box, holly and evergreen oaks. The dark leaves made a backdrop which showed up the women's dresses – lingerie dresses in fine white lawn, or cream and ivory linen – and their lacy parasols, among the crowds that thronged the lawns. The closely mown grass in front of the striped tea tent was criss-crossed with the moving shadows of the guests and among them was a slight wiry figure, like a shadow himself, though his stick was pale against the evergreens.

Leonard Crake.

Connie drew back immediately but she was well hidden. She had expected him to be here. He was here because Ida was here.

He was approaching groups with a cardboard tray of leaflets – probably about the Angels' Charity and the three orphanages – and rattling a tin; Connie could hear the chink of coins from where she stood. The women took the leaflets eagerly and showed them to their husbands; they dropped money into his tin. Everyone wanted to be seen by everyone else as a generous benefactor of the orphaned poor. Connie wondered how much of that money would reach them.

Ida stood beneath a tree on the opposite side from Connie, being talked at by two young men and twirling her parasol in a bored way. Every now and then Leonard Crake would turn his head, more stoat-like than ever, to watch her.

At one point he came close to where Connie was hiding and paused. He didn't see her; he was too busy watching Ida. There was a curious expression in his eyes.

Connie was able to look closely at him, at his scowl and the look in his eyes, and at that moment she understood – almost everything. This afternoon was indeed when it was all going to happen, unless she could do something about it.

She was relieved when he moved away.

'Connie?'

She jumped. Someone had come up behind her in the darkness of the trees.

'Arthur!' With relief she recognised his familiar lanky figure.

He looked flustered. 'Got to start playing in a minute.' He gestured at a red and white striped awning near by; inside she could see an upright piano, with sheet music scattered on the top.

'It's Lady Lamont's piano. Goodness knows how the men carried it in! I was on tenterhooks in case they dropped it.' He looked at her and frowned. 'I thought they'd locked you in?'

'I escaped,' said Connie. Arthur didn't look surprised, or even impressed; his mind was evidently on other things.

'I've spotted Madame Vichani,' he said uneasily. 'She may recognise us. You'd better lie doggo.'

'Why is *she* here?'

'She's been hired to put on a performance. Apparently Lady Lamont attended one of her séances and was impressed.'

As he spoke, Ida's laugh carried to them across the grass.

'It's a pretty poor show,' Arthur said glumly. 'Those two asses are whispering sweet nothings to her and I've got to play the piano and can't see what's going on!'

'She doesn't look as if she's enjoying them much,' said Connie. 'I'll keep an eye on her for you. That's why I'm here, actually.' She didn't like to add '*and to prevent her being murdered*' in case it worried him.

She shrank back behind a tree-trunk as Mr Thurston and Frank passed by the bushes on the other side, close enough for her to lean through the twigs and touch them if she had wanted. But she needn't have worried. Their heads were turned away from her. They were both looking over at Ida and saying something she couldn't hear. She looked for her aunts but couldn't spot them yet.

When she turned back Arthur had gone and within minutes she saw him fold himself on to his piano stool beneath the awning. The hopeful notes of 'Daisy, Daisy, Give Me Your Answer Do' wafted over the crowd.

As people gathered closer to hear, Connie saw Ida enticed over to the tea tent by the two young men. She looked reluctant to go, pretending to laugh as they each took one of her arms, drawing her away from the music. Seconds later Mr Thurston and Frank followed, perhaps by coincidence, perhaps not.

Squeezing through the bushes, Connie darted over to the tea tent after them.

'I'm half crazy, all for the love of you,' carolled Arthur.

Connie entered cautiously, but the tea tent was full and busy. Maids in white aprons rushed about, carrying teapots and trays of cakes. People sat on gold chairs at little round tables. There was a warm, heavy smell of fresh bread, crushed grass and Eau de Cologne.

Neither Mr Thurston nor Frank saw Connie among the crowd; they had had to go right to the back to find a free table.

Connie found herself standing by a larger table covered with flowing white linen. It was laden with plates of sandwiches, scones, meringues and strawberries, and its centrepiece was an enormous fruit cake. Several slices had already been carved from it by a uniformed butler holding a knife with a decorated silver blade. The table was surrounded by guests holding empty plates and standing in a polite, expectant queue; they looked most put out at a small girl's sudden arrival in the middle of them all.

The butler eyed Connie's grubby dress with suspicion as she leaned in and took a sandwich. 'Young lady, are you on your own?'

Lavender appeared behind him, munching a piece of cake. She nodded at the butler. 'It's all right, Higgs. She's a friend of mine.'

The disapproving expressions of the queue were rapidly exchanged for benevolent ones.

'Hello, old sport, enjoying yourself?' Lavender asked Connie.

'Not exactly,' Connie said, helping herself to another sandwich while she could. Peering between two people behind her, she saw Ida sitting with her back to her in a far corner of the tent. The two young men were giving their order to the waitress – and the waitress was none other than Ethel from Madame Vichani's!

Ida had her back to her and Connie couldn't see her shocked expression – for, of course, they would recognise each other. Meanwhile, Mr Thurston and Frank were too deeply engrossed in watching Ida from their table in another corner to spot Connie in the crowd around the cake.

Arthur was playing 'Beautiful Eyes' now. They were all love songs, Connie realised – love songs to Ida, who wouldn't even realise their significance.

'Grub's good,' remarked Lavender. 'Mater supervised it. Pater has lent his special knife from India for cutting the cake.' She leaned closer to Connie and whispered, 'I think Mater's hoping that a rather special guest may turn up. Pity I haven't brought my placard with me!'

'Who is it?'

Lavender put her finger to her lips and grinned. 'I'm sworn to secrecy.'

Arthur launched into the melancholic 'Forlorn, My Love, No Comfort Here'.

The queue round the table began to break up as people carried away their slices of fruit cake. Connie was suddenly exposed.

A young, shrill voice rang out through the tea tent, carrying above the clatter of teacups, the politely muted conversation and even Arthur's playing.

'That girl! Mama, see that girl? She shouldn't be here! She hasn't got a ticket! I bet her people haven't paid!'

27

'Hush, dear,' her embarrassed mother hissed, fanning herself wildly with a tea menu as her daughter pointed an accusing finger at Connie. 'She's with Lady Lavender.'

'But she sneaked in with us! She didn't show a ticket!'

Silence fell.

Eyes swivelled towards Connie, standing by the main table, her mouth bulging with sandwich and her dress still muddy and damp from crawling along the roof. Under the brim of her hat Connie could see that the faces looked unsympathetic.

What was much worse was that from the back of the tea tent two figures suddenly stood up. Mr Thurston and Frank!

Now they were making their way over to her, weaving awkwardly between the small tables, Mr

Thurston tripping over the matting floor. His face was puce with champagne and anger, his hands clenching and unclenching. Frank behind him looked unruffled, but his eyes had narrowed.

Outside, a cry went up suddenly. 'The King! Make way for the King!'

For a few seconds the tent stilled. Teacups remained held in midair, buns halted halfway to mouths. Arthur began to play the National Anthem. Higgs the butler quietly laid down the silver cake knife and stood to attention, his face impassive. As if following his example, everyone else rose from their tables, blocking the way in front of Mr Thurston and Frank.

As the Anthem came to an end, there was a mad rush to the exit. Mothers brandished their daughters like trophies, hoping for the King's approval even before their official court presentation; men followed because they wanted to be seen to be in the right circles: it seemed that everyone was curious to see the King at close quarters.

They trampled past Connie and Lavender, paying them no attention at all, and in the crush Connie lost sight of Mr Thurston and Frank and slipped out herself.

She saw a burly man, surrounded by police and

various officials, approaching with a jaunty step across the grass.

The sun shone on the King's head. She was disappointed to see that he wasn't wearing a crown at all, but a very ordinary top hat like the other gentlemen there, though perhaps rather smoother and silkier than theirs.

'See, I told you!' said Lavender, in Connie's ear.

'But why has he come?'

'Because his lady friend, Mrs Keppel, is on the garden party committee.' Lavender gave a sly smile and nodded in the direction of an auburn-haired woman, considerably younger than the King, who was talking vivaciously to a female guest.

The King was moving along a receiving line of important-looking people, shaking hands and saying a few words. Halfway along he stopped and gestured at Ida, who was standing a little way back. To Connie's disgust she saw that Frank had his arm openly around her waist.

'The King wants to be presented to your cousin!' whispered Lavender.

Ida was gently brought forward by one of the officials, Frank hovering in the background.

Connie glanced behind her and saw that Arthur

had left his piano and was watching Ida, his face anxious. So, it seemed, was the entire garden party, including Aunt Dorothea and Aunt Sylvie, both too intent on Ida and the King to notice her. And Connie, looking around warily for Mr Thurston, couldn't see him either.

To be on the safe side she retreated behind a tree to watch.

'And who are you, my dear?' asked the King, running an appreciative eye over Ida's figure.

'Ida Fairbanks, Your Majesty,' said Ida, opening her beautiful blue eyes very wide and remembering just in time to bob a curtsy.

'Well, Miss Fairbanks,' said the King genially, 'I hope I will have the pleasure of seeing you again at your court presentation?'

Ida looked aghast. 'Blimey, no,' she burst out. 'Not blooming likely!'

A ripple of horror went round the crowd. To swear not only once but twice in public – and in the presence of the King himself! Aunt Dorothea hid her face in her hands.

The King looked surprised for a moment and then threw back his head and guffawed. He twinkled at Ida. 'What a pity, Miss Fairbanks. I would have enjoyed it.'

239

He passed on his way, still chuckling to himself, while the crowd relaxed and laughed politely with him.

Ida was now the girl everyone wanted to meet.

Not only had she been picked out and admired by the King himself, but most of them had seen the recent news stories in the press about the girl who had mysteriously reappeared after so many years. Ida Fairbanks – whose return from the dead the now famous medium Madame Vichani had foretold! It was said that she had even managed to raise Ida's childish spirit at a séance!

As soon as the King had disappeared out of the garden's main gate, taking his entourage with him, people surrounded Ida, wanting introductions, assailing her with a barrage of questions.

Ida looked bewildered and shrank against Frank, who put his arm around her waist and held her to him, crushing her dress.

'It's OK, honey,' he said loudly. 'We'll go home in a minute.'

'Is he your fiancé, Miss Fairbanks?' someone asked.

'No – I mean, yes – I mean, not yet,' stammered Ida.

Frank regarded the crowd with a complacent smile.

'Watch the social columns,' he said and winked, giving Ida a squeeze.

Then Connie saw Arthur stride over and push through to the centre of the crowd. He confronted Frank.

'Take your hands off Miss Fairbanks, you – you utter cad!' he stammered.

Ida looked up at him in amazement. Frank looked taken aback too for a moment, then gave a slow, supercilious smile. 'Oh, it's the music teacher, isn't it?'

'She isn't your fiancée yet! Let go of her, I say!'

'Make me,' said Frank.

'Right!' retorted Arthur and he put up his fists.

Connie bit her lip. Arthur's precious fingers!

'Arthur—' Ida began helplessly.

From all over the garden people gathered to watch, unsure whether this was part of the entertainment or not. The sun went in at that moment and the sky darkened, as if in sympathy with the drama on the grass below.

'Come away, darlings,' a mother said to her two daughters. 'There's going to be a boxing match. I can't think why Lady Lamont thought it would be appropriate.'

Frank let go of Ida and raised his fists, straddling his

feet apart. He looked fit and muscular compared with gangly Arthur. He shook his head at him and smirked.

'OK. You'll see what happens to asses like you!'

Ida gave a cry as he began to dance about in front of Arthur, taunting him, giving little lunges as if he were playing with a puppy.

Arthur dodged and hit out wildly, but his fist went through empty air.

Frank landed a punch on Arthur's arm that must have hurt him. The crowd gave a groan; they appeared to be on Arthur's side, the underdog.

'Take that!' said Arthur undeterred, and he thrust out his fist and hit Frank unexpectedly on the shoulder. He looked amazed at his luck and just managed to dodge another blow from Frank in time.

Then his own fist went out again, an uppercut that landed straight on Frank's jaw.

Frank went over on the grass like a ninepin and lay there spread-eagled, clasping his face and moaning.

A cheer went up from the spectators and Connie cheered with them. They had clearly thought Frank's behaviour with Ida singularly improper in polite society.

Arthur acknowledged the cheer modestly, brushed his hands together and went back to his piano, where he began to play 'To the End of the World with You' with great feeling.

The police by the gates, alerted by the noise, hurried over, but they were too late to establish who had knocked over the man on the ground and Frank was too busy moaning to tell them.

As the men from the St John Ambulance Brigade surrounded Frank, Connie marched over to where Ida was being comforted by her aunts.

'That was all your fault, you know!' she stormed at Ida. 'Arthur might have ruined his piano playing for ever because of you!'

'Connie!' exclaimed Aunt Dorothea. 'Whatever are you doing here? Uncle Harold said—'

'How can you love that bounder —' Connie went on, gesturing at Frank's recumbent body '— when Arthur is worth ten million times more? Don't you understand that he loves you, Ida?'

Ida stared at her for a moment with her mouth open, then burst into loud sobs. Gathering up her dress, she ran clumsily away from the three of them, across the lawn towards the east gate.

Connie looked after her in dismay. 'I didn't mean to upset her. Shall I go after her?'

Aunt Dorothea put a restraining hand on Connie's

arm. 'She's going back to Alfred Place. It's best to leave her alone at home for a while.'

So she needn't worry just yet about Ida being murdered, thought Connie. That was a relief.

'Perhaps I shouldn't have told her about Arthur,' she said. 'But he does love her, you know.'

'We know, dear, but *she* didn't realise about him until the fight a moment ago,' said Aunt Sylvie, smiling beatifically after Ida's retreating figure. 'She's been in love with him for some time.'

'Has she?' said Connie, in astonishment.

Aunt Dorothea took her arm. 'But the most important thing now is to avoid your Uncle Harold!'

It was easier said than done.

As Lavender's mother announced through a megaphone that Madame Vichani, the celebrated medium, would be starting her session in five minutes, Connie saw to her horror that Mr Thurston had spotted her once again from where he had been standing, beneath the far trees of the garden.

28

It began to spit with rain from a black sky. As people hurried for the shelter of Madame Vichani's tent, Mr Thurston moved towards Connie, his teeth bared, his thick arms swinging by his sides. He looked quite mad at that moment and she felt horribly afraid.

But it seemed that because of Ida Mr Thurston was a celebrity in his own right. Well-wishers came up to him, slapped him on the back, congratulated him. 'Your stepdaughter ... After so many years ... Remarkable . . . Noticed by the King himself!'

He flapped at them furiously. 'Out of my way!' Putting his hands around his mouth, he bawled out, 'CONSTANCE! Come here!' Then he seemed to recollect himself. 'Apologies, my step-niece—'

But his step-niece, accompanied by his wife, was already at the opening of the main tent.

Looking back as she entered, Connie saw that Aunt

Sylvie had wandered across to him, snapping her umbrella up over her head. No doubt she had foreseen the rain.

'Harold, would you be so kind as to escort me to the tea tent?' her voice quavered back to Connie, sounding remarkably older than her years. 'I am gasping for a cup of tea!'

Mr Thurston knew he could not ignore Aunt Sylvie's request in front of so many. Connie thought she could hear his growl of frustration as he took her aunt's arm.

The interior of Madame Vichani's tent, with all the flaps pegged down, was warm and dim, made even darker by the overcast sky outside. Great swags of blue and silver silk hid the canvas walls and the air was richly fragrant with the white lilies that decorated the tent poles.

They reminded Connie of funerals and she immediately thought of her dead parents and felt a little sick. There had been flowers like these scattered on their coffins. It was the first time she had realised she truly was an orphan.

The tent was already almost filled with an expectant audience, who didn't seem to mind that they had to sit on hard collapsible chairs: there might be thrilling new revelations from Madame Vichani this afternoon and anyway they were now out of the rain. The persistent drumming of it on the canvas roof above them only added to the gothic atmosphere.

In front of them was a wooden platform with three steps leading up to it. On this makeshift stage there was a small table that was covered by a dark blue cloth decorated with stars. A single gold chair had been placed at either end of the table.

The audience stared at the chairs speculatively and whispered to each other.

Connie and Aunt Dorothea found two vacant seats halfway down the rows; one was an aisle seat and Connie took it, looking around surreptitiously. It was important that certain people were there in the audience.

Yes – she had spotted Leonard Crake, sitting a little way along the row in front, with his tray of leaflets on his knee, and she could see that the hard-eyed woman in a matron's uniform next to him was Mrs Goodenough. Lavender and her society friends were sitting in the row in front. Lavender craned round as Connie and her aunt squeezed in, and winked at Connie.

Then Arthur edged along Connie's row and sat down with a sigh on an empty chair beyond Aunt Dorothea.

Connie felt a quiver of sympathy. 'She loves you, you know!' she hissed across Aunt Dorothea, but Arthur made no sign that he had heard.

Lady Lamont, wearing a hat of a violent and unmissable shade of purple, advanced towards the steps and mounted the stage. She had as powerful a voice as her daughter's and it carried easily above the noise of the rain. She fixed the audience with a penetrating eye.

'My lords, ladies and gentlemen, we are gathered here today in an excellent cause. The three orphanages that the Angels' Charity befriend are all deserving and through our benevolence have been able to provide for the orphans in their care. It is your generosity that has enabled . . .'

Connie had found Aunt Sylvie amongst the sea of faces behind her. Her aunt sat alone in the back row, looking dreamily at her feet. Mr Thurston stood with other late-comers by the single open flap of the tent. He looked straight back at at Connie, his face thunderous. She turned round to the front quickly, her heart thumping.

Lady Lamont was finishing her speech.

'And now, my friends, this is what we have all been waiting for: our own special session with the famous Madame Vichani, who has kindly agreed to waive her fee today. Many of you may indeed have attended Madame Vichani's sessions, as I have, but she will be known to all of you from the newspapers as a gifted medium.

'It was she who intercepted a message from the spirit world foretelling the return of the heiress, Miss Ida Fairbanks, whom some of you may have met today. A beautiful young girl, safely restored to her family after missing so mysteriously for many years.'

Aunt Dorothea took out a lace handkerchief and dabbed at her eyes, while the audience muttered and nodded and heads turned, looking for Ida. Connie noticed that several people she knew were also searching amongst the faces: Leonard Crake, Mrs Goodenough and Mr Thurston. Arthur sat with his head bowed, his fingers pleating his trousers.

'And so now without further ado I'd like to introduce – Madame Vichani!' said Lady Lamont, with a welcoming smile, and she flourished a white-gloved hand in the direction of the tent opening. Those late-comers standing there parted, to allow the medium to progress through.

People began to clap automatically and then fell silent.

Madame Vichani swayed up the aisle, clad from head to foot in a flowing silver gown. She carried a candle in a silver candlestick, which reflected up into her grave, downcast face and made rippling reflections in her gown as she moved. Her long hair shone golden in the light and lifted as she walked.

Goodness! thought Connie. She looks exactly as if she's going to bed!

But others in the audience were impressed. A murmur of awe arose, quickly hushed, as she slowly mounted the steps to the stage. With care she placed the candlestick on the table and turned to the audience, spreading her arms wide so that her sleeves looked like the silver wings of some exotic bird.

She began to intone in a low chant that was surprisingly mesmeric. It might have been coincidence, but at that moment the drumming on the canvas roof died to a meek patter.

'I am here this afternoon because I wish to help. It is not only poor orphans who require help: all of us yearn after spiritual reassurance. I have a unique gift of clairvoyance. By contact alone I can bring messages to you from those you thought dead, or see into your

250

future. When I sit at this table —' she touched it with a finger '— and look into the candle flame I can see images that tell me who you are.

'Now —' she said, her voice soft yet carrying '— give me a moment to receive the vibrations from those I may be able to help.'

She sat down and was still and silent for some moments. No one in the audience stirred. It was if she had laid a spell on them all.

All, except Connie. She watched closely, curious to see how Madame Vichani would deceive so many.

Then Madame Vichani rose and pointed at someone in the front row. 'You, my dear, come and sit up here with me.'

There was hesitation and then a girl rose and went to the stage. When she sat down Connie recognised her again. Ethel, Madame Vichani's maid! She was dressed as she had been while waitressing in the tea tent, in a frilled apron, black dress and white cap.

'Give me your hand,' said Madame Vichani.

The candlelight flickered on the two hands, clasped together. There was a long pause while Madame Vichani stared into the naked yellow flame.

'You have lost someone dear to you recently,' said

Madame Vichani, in tones of great sympathy.

Ethel nodded and gave a sob. 'Me Pa.'

Ethel was not a good actress, not nearly as good as Ida had been. Madame Vichani must have been sorry to lose Ida. Yet still the audience leaned forward, craning to hear.

'I believe I am getting through to him,' said Madame Vichani, after another long silence. 'He always wore a red neck handkerchief. Is that correct?'

Another sob from Ethel. 'Yes, ma'm.'

'He is well, my dear, and happy, and does not want you to dwell on his death any more. Be at peace is his message.'

'Oh, oh!' cried Ethel and she fled from the stage, relieved, no doubt, that her act was over.

Madame Vichani smiled and looked at the audience. 'Let me pick out my next visitor.' Her finger wavered and steadied. 'In the third row, four seats along. Would you come up, please?'

A young girl, with what looked like a pink meringue on her head, climbed the steps reluctantly and sat down, blushing. She offered her right hand and Madame Vichani took it and held it, while the girl giggled nervously and Madame Vichani stared at the candle flame.

At last Madame Vichani said, 'I see trees arching overhead.'

'Trees?' said the girl, frowning.

'Wait – not trees. A roof, the roof of a great cathedral. You are below, walking up the aisle, dressed in white, and there is a young man waiting for you at the altar.'

'Charlie!' breathed the girl.

'I see a long, happy marriage. You will both be prosperous. I see babies, too . . .'

Madame Vichani would have recognised the Honourable Cynthia Cardew from her engagement picture in the papers. Cynthia was engaged to a wealthy young merchant banker, though Connie couldn't remember his name. Indeed, for all Connie knew, Madame Vichani had seen a guest list for today, or known that Cynthia's mother was on the Angels' Charity committee.

However, Cynthia was thrilled. She rose to her feet, clasping her hands together. An enormous emerald ring on her left hand caught the light. 'Thank you!' she stuttered and returned to her seat.

Next, Madame Vichani picked out an old man who could hardly dodder up the steps to the stage he was so bow-legged, and had to be helped by two equally elderly gentleman. She gave him reassurances about 'his estate left in good hands', 'friends waiting to welcome', 'hunting to hounds for eternity across the Elysian Fields'.

His friends clapped him on the back at that, and he nearly collapsed on stage.

He was probably one of the donors to the Angels' Charity, whose name would have appeared on the list. Madame Vichani had done her homework and scrutinised it closely.

Then Madame Vichani made her great mistake. She picked out Lavender.

She would have seen Lavender mentioned in the press as a suffragette, read about the row between her and her father, and though Lavender's mother was Chairwoman of the Garden Party committee, Madame Vichani must have thought it would be easy to hoodwink the audience into thinking she had known nothing at all about Lavender until this moment.

Lavender bunched up her skirts and sat down. She thrust out her hand, which Madame Vichani took. She gazed into the candle flame.

'Fire away!' said Lavender.

A pause. 'I see words carried in the air, broken bottles, crowds,' said Madame Vichani, in a slow, thoughtful voice. 'I hear angry voices. There is a rift in your family. This is not the right path for you. You are torn—'

Lavender snatched her hand away and leaped to her feet, pushing the table away. Her red hair blazed and so did she.

'This is utter tosh! You've heard about me, perhaps from my mother, or from the newspapers.' She addressed the audience. 'You've all been taken in! Is there no one here who can expose this charlatan?'

Connie jumped up. This was her chance. Her clear young voice rang across the tent.

'Me! I've been investigating Madame Vichani for a while!'

Laughter rippled through the audience as everyone stared at Connie. Undeterred, Connie remained standing and glared around challengingly under her hat.

Lavender beckoned to her. 'Then come on up!'

Aunt Dorothea clutched Connie's hand. 'Oh, Connie, you've gone too far this time!'

Lady Lamont looked as if she didn't know whether to be amused or furious at her daughter's challenge to the audience, let alone Connie's audacity. She opted to look indulgent, but her face clearly found it a struggle.

'My name is Constance Clementine Carew,' Connie called out, as she stepped into the aisle, 'and I am Miss Ida Fairbanks's cousin!'

A fascinated silence fell, apart from a few shocked gasps, a few titters, as she marched up the aisle to the steps. It appeared that everyone was curious to see what this precocious child cousin might say about the beautiful Miss Fairbanks's extraordinary reappearance. Perhaps, too, they needed a little amusement after Madame Vichani's pronouncements. They were willing to be indulgent; they sat back and waited to be entertained.

Connie reached the stage and stared out at the audience, holding herself as tall and straight as was possible for a twelve-year-old of somewhat short stature.

People glanced at each other with tolerant smiles and gazed back. Connie hoped it was her dignity and poise that held their attention, but in any case she was going to make sure she kept it.

Lavender grinned at her.

'*Over to you, Connie Carew!*' she sang out and left Connie standing alone on the stage.

29

Connie took off her hat and laid it on the table while she thought what she was going to say.

'You!' said Madame Vichani, through gritted teeth.

'Madame Vichani and I have met before,' Connie announced to the audience. 'I'd suspected for some time that she might be a fraud and I was right!' This raised sceptical laughter, but she persevered.

'She chooses orphans who can't stay on at the Sisters of Hope in Hammersmith because they're too old. She pretends she's employing them as housemaids in her house in Pelham Crescent, but in fact she teaches them to act in her séances. They're dressed like spirits and come up from the basement through a trapdoor in her cabinet.'

The laughter had died, but there were mutters of disbelief in the audience, which Connie ignored.

'I went to a séance with my aunts, and a girl in a

shining dress appeared. My poor aunt thought she was Ida, her long-lost daughter. She said she was "coming home". Then the same girl turned up at our house.'

Somewhere a woman began to cry. Connie knew it was her own dear Aunt Dorothea but this was something she had to do.

Madame Vichani had risen to her feet, her face ugly with fury. 'How dare you? You, a mere child, know nothing of the spirit world! Where is your proof for all this?'

'I have a witness,' said Connie calmly. 'Arthur Harker, would you stand up?'

Arthur rose to his feet, looking startled and shaken. Connie willed him to be brave.

He stood, speechless. The audience waited breathlessly and so did Connie.

'It's true,' he said at last and his voice grew stronger. 'Everything Connie has said is true. Connie and I went to another séance later and Madame Vichani locked us in for spying on her. It was her maid Ethel who was pretending to be a spirit this time.' He pointed at Ethel in her waitress costume, shrinking into her seat in the front row. 'But later she was jolly plucky and helped us escape.'

'Ethel, will you back us up?' said Connie, as

astonishment stirred through the audience. 'You helped us then and it was very brave of you. Can you be brave again and help us now?'

Ethel looked hesitant. She could lose her job. But she was flattered to be described as brave. Now it seemed she had an important new role as witness. Most significant of all, as Connie knew, she heartily disliked Madame Vichani. She would be conscious that all eyes were on her, all these important people harking to her every word. She would hope that one of these society ladies would offer her a position in the future.

Connie waited patiently, knowing what she was thinking.

Ethel jumped up from her seat, snatched off her waitress cap and began to untie her apron.

'Mrs Brown's a rotten employer,' she burst out, throwing them down on the matting floor. 'That's what her real name is for those who wants to know. She's no better than any of us, no miracle links to the other world. The little girl's right! It was all deception and I was there, pretending to be dead souls returned. But I'm a good housemaid, I am!'

'How dare you?' hissed Madame Vichani, amid an explosion of laughter. 'This is all untrue! How can you insult my gift in such a way?'

'Thank you, Ethel,' said Connie.

She gazed out over the audience, which had fallen silent. No one knew how to react. No one dared look at their hostess, Lady Lamont. But this was even better entertainment than the séance they had been expecting.

'I'm going to talk about the girl known as my cousin, Ida Fairbanks, now,' announced Connie.

'She was taken in by the Sisters of Hope at two years old, the same age Ida Fairbanks was when she went missing. Ida Fairbanks was wearing a gold locket at the time, engraved with her first name and date of birth. But there was no mention of this locket in the orphanage register. Yet when the girl who called herself Ida came to our house, she had the locket with her.'

People leaned forward, craning to hear. Connie raised her voice.

'So there were two possibilities: first, that this girl really was Ida Fairbanks, or that she had stolen the locket and was an imposter. You see, Ida Fairbanks was due to inherit a large fortune on her eighteenth birthday and that was very soon.'

Now there was utter silence. The rain had stopped.

Far away a horse whinnied amongst the carriages waiting outside the square garden, but otherwise Connie knew that she had the audience enthralled.

Madame Vichani sat slumped in her seat, shaking her head as if to deny everything, her expression bitter. Word of today's exposure would spread. She would never be able to practise in London society again. She had been foiled by a twelve-year-old and she would take her revenge one day.

Connie could see these thoughts mirrored in Madame Vichani's ravaged, rouged face, but she could not spare any sympathy for her. Besides, she had not finished with her yet.

'If the girl who had arrived at our house was truly Ida Fairbanks, then why had she been working at Madame Vichani's? Had she come to us by coincidence, in reply to our cook's advertisement for an under-maid, or had she been sent by Madame Vichani? Madame Vichani knew about the inheritance from the newspaper stories at the time. Perhaps she had persuaded the girl to pretend to be Ida Fairbanks and share the fortune with her!'

Madame Vichani sat rigid, her face expressionless now.

Connie looked out, clear-eyed, at the audience.

'Ladies and gentlemen, on the day little Ida Fairbanks went missing fifteen years ago, her nursemaid had taken her to Kensington Gardens as usual. The nursemaid, Sadie Turner, was being courted by a man named Leonard Crake, who used to sit with Sadie in the park. They sat together that afternoon and later little Ida disappeared.'

Connie allowed a significant pause for the audience to take this in, then continued.

'When the girl calling herself Ida first arrived at our house, Leonard Crake followed us. He also followed me and threatened me when I was alone. His wife says he is violent. For a long time I wondered how he fitted into the story, but now I know.'

Connie could see Leonard Crake in the audience. His face was wooden, but he was gnawing his nails with his long yellow teeth as if he would like to bite Connie too.

She took a deep breath. This was her greatest gamble.

'Leonard Crake,' she said slowly. 'Would you come up here, please?'

30

He was cornered. Like a feral animal Leonard Crake looked to left and right and saw no help from the well-fed Society faces there, eyes gleaming with excited curiosity. Slowly he got to his feet and went reluctantly to the steps. He left his stick behind, but appeared to have no difficulty in walking or climbing up to the stage.

'I warned you to keep out of this,' he hissed at Connie. 'Bad things will happen now.'

'I know,' said Connie quietly. 'But you won't be part of them, will you, Mr Crake? That's all in the past.' She gestured at the tray of leaflets, still hanging round his neck. 'You work for charity, doing good, isn't that right?'

They might have been having a private conversation together, but for the rows of faces, staring at them.

'So I won't be in trouble?' he hissed at her. 'There

are coppers everywhere!'

'It will help if you tell the truth.'

She gazed at him and after a second or two he nodded. Madame Vichani sagged lower in her seat.

'I'm going to ask you some questions, Mr Crake,' said Connie, raising her voice again so the audience could hear. 'Would you answer as loudly as you can? At the time of Ida's disappearance you'd done some really bad things, hadn't you?'

He scowled. 'Yes, miss. But I went to prison for them later. I did my time.'

A thrill of horror went through the audience to think they were so close to a self-confessed crook. Now they were more fascinated than ever.

'People came to you when they needed special "jobs" done, didn't they? One day someone came to you and asked you to get rid of a little girl. It's easy to murder a two-year-old, isn't it? And you were promised a very large fee.'

Crake nodded, but began to protest. Connie held up her hand. The audience scarcely breathed.

'To do it you needed help. You had to tell the little girl's nanny. You promised her a share of the fee, and marriage. And so she agreed. She didn't fall asleep that hot afternoon as she told everyone later, but watched you carry little Ida off to her fate. Is that right?'

Crake nodded.

'So what happened then, Mr Crake?'

He faced Connie dumbly, his eyes desperate. A sound came out of his mouth that made no sense. Those nearest the stage saw tears begin to stream down his face, catching the candlelight.

'Tell us, Mr Crake,' said Connie gently.

He shook his head.

'You couldn't do it, could you?' said Connie. 'You carried Ida away in your arms and you took her to the Sisters of Hope.'

'She was so beautiful,' he burst out. 'How could I kill such a pretty little thing? I'd planned the murder all right. I was going to take her back to my lodging and strangle her, then dump the body. But when it came to it, I couldn't do it. She looked so perfect, asleep in my arms. I never told Sadie. She always thought I'd done it. But I didn't. I took her to the orphanage and they took her in and I've watched over her ever since, I have, watched her growing up all this time. I've protected her like a father!'

'So you shared the murder payment with Sadie and then as time passed you realised you could get some money from Ida's inheritance as well,' said Connie. She kept her voice steady, betraying no accusation. Whatever happened she didn't want Crake to flee before she had finished.

'Mrs Goodenough, the head matron at the Sisters of Hope, knew who Ida was because of the gold locket you had forgotten to take off. When the story of the little missing heiress came out in the newspapers the next day, she put two and two together. She didn't enter the locket in the register on purpose. Perhaps she had already planned what might happen in the future. For her great friend was Madame Vichani, and Mrs Goodenough arranged for Ida to work for her when she left the orphanage.'

Connie looked down at the medium. 'You put your card through our door deliberately, hoping we'd come to a séance. It was an extra stroke of luck when we did, wasn't it?'

Madame Vichani did not respond; she was beaten and she knew it.

'At that séance Ida was quickly told what to say and then a little later she was sent to our house in Alfred Street West. The timing was right: her eighteenth birthday was coming up, when she would inherit the Fairbanks fortune.

'You were also in that plot, Mr Crake! You, Madame Vichani here and Mrs Goodenough, manipulated Ida and promised her a quarter of the fortune. Only it was wholly hers by right, wasn't it? I don't know what you said to make Ida agree to it, but I know she can't have wanted to. She still doesn't realise that she isn't an imposter at all!'

Connie looked sternly at Leonard Crake. 'So it's not quite true to say that you have turned over a new leaf, is it?'

Crake stood sullenly in front of Connie, his tears dry, his stance aggressive.

'I took care of Ida, didn't I? Always in the Sisters, doing odd jobs so I could keep an eye on her. I saw her safely into your house. I never murdered her. I protected her, like a father would! It wasn't my fault things turned out the way they did.'

Connie took a deep breath.

'So who bribed you to murder Ida, Mr Crake? My Aunt Sylvie said that it was a man who made Sadie Turner look "a little slip of a thing" when he handed over the money. That man wasn't you at all, Mr Crake, but a much bigger, bulkier man, fed on red roast beef, not scraps from the gutter.

'It was someone who knew he would be able to get

his hands on the Fairbanks fortune if Ida never claimed it. Someone who desperately needed that money because of his gambling habit and because his business was doing badly, even then. Someone who knew the girl who came to the family house that day must be an imposter because he thought she had been murdered by his orders! But he wasn't going to tell because he wanted his son to marry her and share the Fairbanks fortune with him.

'How could you send Ida back to the very place where she was in the greatest danger, Mr Crake?' said Connie fiercely. 'That person is here in the audience, isn't he?'

Leonard Crake stretched out his arm and pointed a finger. The finger swayed over the rapt audience and then fell.

'He was here,' muttered Leonard Crake. 'Where's he gone, then?'

The space at the back of the tent where Harold Thurston had been standing was empty.

31

When had Mr Thurston disappeared? Early on, Connie was sure. He hadn't vanished because of her accusations – perhaps he had never heard them.

He was after Ida and she was alone in the house in Alfred Place West. In the madness of his mind she was the only thing that stood between him and the Fairbanks fortune.

Connie gave a horrified glance at Leonard Crake, then she fled down the steps from the stage. She ran to the row where she had been sitting.

'Come on, Arthur! Ida's in danger!'

She was aware of her aunt's white, frightened face but there was no time to explain.

Arthur looked bewildered. 'Where to?'

'Back to Alfred Place! We've got to rescue Ida!'

Still bewildered, he rose from his seat and stumbled after her. Behind them the audience was in uproar, people turning to each other in confusion.

Connie did not look back to see what had happened to Madame Vichani, or to Leonard Crake, as they broke through into the damp air, ahead of the people beginning to flood out amid a hubbub of excited chatter.

Frank was no longer lying on the grass; he must have been taken off by the ambulance men, probably suffering from concussion.

But Frank didn't concern Connie. She was much more worried by the sight of Higgs the butler, who had arrived back at the tea tent and was waving his arms in alarm.

'The cake knife's gone! Stolen while I was in the séance!'

Connie made straight for the east gate across the wet grass; it was the gate closest to Alfred Place West. For once she was thankful that she still wore a knee-length dress and could run easily.

The policeman at the gate looked at her in astonishment. 'Everything all right, miss?'

'No!' gasped Connie. 'Someone's about to be murdered in Alfred Place West! You let a man through – he had a knife from the tea tent under his coat!'

'Theft, is it?' he said. 'Righto, miss! I'll summon

some colleagues. We'll follow you.'

Connie sprinted on as the sound of the policeman's whistle shrilled through the damp air. She was aware that Arthur was following her as fast as he could but poor Arthur was awkward and not at all athletic.

Footsteps pounded on her heels. She reached Alfred Place and glanced back, to check how close Arthur was behind her.

It was Frank! There was a bandage round his jaw and above it his eyes glared at her.

'How did you get out of your room, you little devil?' he spluttered through the bandage. He hadn't been in the séance, he couldn't have heard what she said about his father, but he was gaining on her and Arthur was far behind.

Robert from next door had come out on to his steps, perhaps alerted by all the commotion on the quiet pavements of Alfred Place. He twirled the hatbox by its string in a hopeful way.

'Stop him, Robert!' panted Connie. She gestured behind her.

Robert, to his credit, obeyed immediately. As Connie raced past, he dropped the hatbox, nipped down the steps and stuck out his foot in its shiny black shoe in front of Frank.

Frank saw the foot, dodged to avoid it and slipped over on the wet pavement. He lay sprawled on his back, the bandage now over one eye.

'You ruddy little blighter!' he shouted at Robert, who pulled a rude face at him and charged after Connie, eager for more adventure.

Connie hurled herself up the steps of her house and pounded on the front door. It was fast shut and she didn't have a key. She took hold of the knocker and slammed it several times against the wood.

'Bessie! Bessie!'

Bessie, opened the front door, duster in hand, looking startled and alarmed. She stared at Connie, at the unfamiliar boy standing next to her and then at Arthur, who had caught up at last. The top step was suddenly crowded, blocking Bessie's view of Frank on the pavement.

'Miss Constance! Whatever's the matter? Just look at the state of your dress!'

'Where's Ida?' said Connie urgently.

'Miss Ida is upstairs in her room, resting,' said Bessie primly. 'And if I'm not mistaken, you were supposed to be in your room too, miss!'

'Where's Mr Thurston?'

'I thought he was at the garden party.' She stopped

as she caught sight of the pavement below, where three policemen were now mistakenly searching a furious Frank for the knife.

'Gracious, the police! What's Master Frank gone and done?'

Of course. Mr Thurston had his own front-door key. He would have let himself in.

Connie darted past Bessie. 'I'll explain later!'

'Oh, no, you don't,' said Bessie to Robert, who tried to barge after Connie. 'Nor you, Mr Harker! It's not your day here.' She gave a last shocked look at the struggle on the pavement and slammed the front door smartly.

Connie only half took in that her comrades were no longer with her but she was in too much of a hurry to stop.

It seemed dark inside the house, as it always did.

Bessie disappeared into the dining-room with her duster, shaking her head and muttering, 'The police! I never! Good thing you didn't get mixed up with the likes of *him*, Bessie my girl!'

Connie ran down the length of the hall to the

staircase. Only then did she stop and listen.

Above her the house groaned, its timbers swelling with the damp evening; the cistern gurgled in the bathroom on the second floor. She couldn't hear any human sound but it was a tall house with a deep and muffling stairwell. Then she caught the faintest smell of macassar hair oil.

Mr Thurston was definitely back.

She flew up the stairs, past the first floor with the drawing-room and Mr Thurston's morning-room. Bessie had left the doors open after cleaning and a glance told her that the rooms were empty. Then the bedrooms on the next floor: Aunt Dorothea's bedroom and Mr Thurston's dressing-room, where Frank had been sleeping.

She tried to make her feet as quiet as possible on the stairs but the carpet became so threadbare as she went up the house that they clattered on the wood beneath. It grew darker as she ran up and she wished Bessie had lit the gas lights. The damp patches on the walls loomed at her, as if they were closing in.

It wasn't until she reached the shadowy landing between Ida and Aunt Sylvie's bedrooms and had to stop for breath that she became aware of two things.

Ida's bedroom door was wide open, her bed empty

and it looked as if there had been a struggle in there. But then Ida's room was always untidy. Perhaps, after all—

Then Connie heard someone – or two people – on the top landing above her.

32

The familiar, eerie creak of Mr Thurston's corset came to her first, then she heard him panting for breath. She stood hidden in the doorway of Ida's bedroom and looked up.

He and Ida were struggling together, swaying in the half-light. Mr Thurston was hampered by holding the knife in one hand, which he was trying to bring closer to Ida's throat. His hold on it slipped and it fell down the stairwell, past Connie, gleaming as it fell. She heard it land somewhere below her.

But now Mr Thurston was free to grip both Ida's forearms and he began to push her slowly but surely towards the open staircase. He was unfit but he was a big man and much stronger than Ida. Connie realised what he wanted to do: he would make her death from a fall look like an accident.

Ida's hair had fallen down around her shoulders.

Oddly, she made no sound. It was Mr Thurston who did: grunting and groaning as she kicked out at him.

'Let go of Ida, do you hear?' Connie shouted up.

He didn't even pause. It was as if, in his crazed desire for Ida's death, he hadn't heard her at all. She started towards the stairs, not knowing what she would do but determined to rescue Ida somehow.

As she did so, a figure brushed by and darted up the last flight before she could – a man, shadowy and agile by habit, used to giving the law the slip, whose past in the criminal underworld had never truly left him.

'If you harm a hair of her head, Thurston,' said Leonard Crake, 'I'll beat you into yesteryear!'

Mr Thurston, distracted, must have loosened his grip on Ida. With a muffled moan, she slid to the landing floor. The two men confronted each other over her prone body, Mr Thurston still panting with the effort of holding her.

There was a second's pause and then Crake went for Mr Thurston. Thurston tried to dodge the raised blows, but he was portly and gasping for breath.

He tried to make a run for the stairs, perhaps already dizzy from pain. Something happened then – Connie was never sure what it was, because she couldn't make out what exactly was going on in the shadows above her – but it seemed that his foot must have caught in one of the holes in the carpet near the bannister rail.

He clutched at the rail for support and with a terrible splintering of wood it broke and Mr Thurston plunged through and down the stairwell, all the way down the tall, tall house to the hall.

Leonard Crake bent over Ida's still body. His voice drifted down to Connie.

'Farewell, my angel.'

Connie became aware that through this there had been a tremendous knocking on the front door. At some point Bessie must have opened it, for Arthur, Robert and a policeman were there on the landing with her.

Robert looked a little wild-eyed. 'I've never seen a dead body before.'

'Did you see what happened, miss?' asked the policeman.

To Connie's surprise she was trembling all over. 'Is he dead?'

'I'm afraid so,' said the policeman sympathetically.

'It's a long way to fall. We'll have to examine the accident area later and talk to you. Was he your father, miss?'

'No,' said Connie. 'No, he was my step-uncle and please could you remove his corpse before my aunt arrives?'

'I'm afraid we can't do that. She'll have to identify him.' He squinted up into the shadows above and frowned. 'Is that another body on the landing?'

'It's my cousin. She's only fainted.'

'Must be the shock. You'd better see to her. We'll want to talk to her later.' He patted Connie on the back. 'Brace up, miss. You're a plucky little thing, I can see that.'

Connie looked around for Arthur for reassurance, but love had lent him new powers: he leaped up the stairs in a surprisingly athletic way and knelt beside Ida.

'My darling! Speak to me!'

The policeman disappeared down the stairs. When Connie found her legs could move again she went up after Arthur.

Robert followed her gallantly. 'Do you mind about your step-uncle being dead?' he whispered.

Connie shook her head. Now wasn't the right

moment to explain how evil Mr Thurston had been.

She looked around for Leonard Crake, but he was nowhere to be seen. Somehow he had slipped through the house invisibly, a shadow passing over the walls, merging with the damp patches. His old habits in the presence of police had never left him.

Ida, her face white as alabaster, was slumped by the broken bannisters.

Arthur wrung his hands. He had, at least, removed the handkerchief Mr Thurston had stuffed in her mouth to stop her screams.

'What shall I do?' he said, in desperation to Connie. 'She won't wake up!'

'Is she dead too?' asked Robert, rather pale.

'Of course not!' said Connie crossly. 'Turn her on her side, Arthur, and tell her you love her!'

In the end it took the three of them to heave Ida over – she was no longer quite as ethereal as she had been when she first arrived at Alfred Place West – and then Connie nudged Robert to stand back discreetly.

As far as Arthur was concerned, he needed no hints as to what to do.

He bent down over Ida's recumbent figure and said loudly in her ear, 'Ida, my dearest, will you marry me? I adore you above all things, even my piano.'

Ida's long lashes fluttered. She coughed. Pink came back into her cheeks. She stretched and smiled painfully up at him. Her slender arms were bruised beneath the torn chiffon. Her voice came out as a strange croak.

'You're a perfectly splendid fellow, Arthur, and of course I'll blooming marry you!' Then she put her hand to her mouth. 'Oh, dear, but I can't! I've just remembered why!'

'Why?' said Arthur, stricken.

'Because I've lied to everyone all the time I've been here! I've pretended to be Ida Fairbanks when I'm not. I took everyone in, except Connie. You see, you're much too good for me, Arthur dear!' And she began to weep.

'Stop that,' said Connie sternly. 'You *are* Ida Fairbanks! I've just proved it at the garden party and if only you hadn't run away like that you would have heard me say so!'

Ida blinked. 'I *am* Ida Fairbanks?'

Connie nodded. 'I'm sorry I didn't believe you.'

'But,' said Ida, in a pitifully small voice, 'it doesn't take away from the fact that I thought I wasn't and I lied that I was and I was going to take the inheritance – oh, it's all so confusing!'

'We forgive you, don't we, Arthur?' said Connie.

'Oh, yes, rather!' said Arthur.

'Well, in that case I will marry you, Arthur Harker!'

'You don't love Frank, then?' he said tremulously.

'Frank? I can't believe I ever thought that dreadful man was a friend! It's you I've always loved, Arthur. But you never said anything to me, so I thought . . .'

Arthur was couldn't say anything at all now, he was so overcome. He took Ida's hand and stroked it.

'I tried to run from Mr Thurston,' whispered Ida. 'I thought if I reached Connie's room I could lock the door on him. But I'd forgotten it was already locked!'

'Hush, my dearest,' said Arthur. 'Don't think about it any more. That man is gone for ever.'

'I don't think you should move for a while after fainting like that,' said Connie to Ida. 'Arthur will look after you.'

Arthur appeared very happy to do so. He began to kiss Ida tenderly.

Robert looked at him in disgust. 'Can we leave all this soppy stuff now,' he said to Connie, 'and see what's happening downstairs?'

Downstairs, there was no sign of dead Mr Thurston, which was a relief. He must have been removed already.

More policemen had arrived and were milling about in the hall, talking to Bessie, who looked as if she were enjoying being the centre of attention. Tactfully, they avoided Aunt Dorothea and Aunt Sylvie.

Aunt Dorothea was sitting on the chair next to the telephone table and Aunt Sylvie was sitting on the stairs, skirts spread wide and legs apart in their sturdy woollen stockings. Not even a garden party had made her change out of them.

She grasped Connie's ankle as she went past.

'Well done, dear girl!' she hissed. 'Of course I knew that ridiculous medium woman was a fake at the very beginning. I shall tell the police so! I do wish they'd hurry up and talk to me.'

Connie went over to Aunt Dorothea. She was sitting, looking shocked but dignified, her hands clasped in her lap over her beautiful tea gown.

'Poor Harold,' she murmured to Connie. 'I told him we needed a new stair carpet.'

Connie put her arms around her. 'I'm so sorry, Aunt.'

Her aunt was rigid in her embrace. 'I'm not,' said

Aunt Dorothea. 'He was a bully. He bullied all of us. I should have stood up for you, Connie, but I never did.'

'It doesn't matter now.'

'And what has happened to darling Ida? Where is she? Is she all right? It will be such a shock for her.'

'She'll be coming down shortly, I expect.'

Aunt Dorothea would not know that Mr Thurston had tried to murder Ida before he died and perhaps it was best left like that. Connie couldn't help feeling pain that even now her aunt should put Ida first. But, of course, Ida was her daughter. Whereas Connie . . .

'Where's Frank? He must be told that his father is dead.'

'I'm not sure,' said Connie carefully.

She felt a touch on her shoulder.

'I say, I've never seen so many policemen in one place!' said Robert. He looked thrilled. Then he took in Aunt Dorothea's expression and pulled himself together.

'I'm so sorry for your loss,' he said to her, with a solemn bow.

Perhaps realising this might be the right moment to leave, he stuck out his right hand to Connie.

'It's been topping meeting you, Connie Carew! Good thing I've got big feet, isn't it?' They shook hands gravely. 'I could come round tomorrow,' he remarked, in an offhand way. 'I'll give your route a go,' and he gave her a small, secretive smile.

'What a nice, polite boy,' said Aunt Dorothea vaguely, looking after his departing back. 'I'm glad you're finding friends, Connie.'

'Sorry to bother you, miss,' said a policeman to Connie. 'But I wonder if I might have a word in private?'

Connie followed him into the dining-room and then looked back, alerted by Ida's voice.

Ida was running down the stairs, her skirts hitched up, her fair hair tumbling around her shoulders. She looked radiant and an awestruck silence fell over the policemen gathered below.

'Mother! Mother!'

She ran straight to Aunt Dorothea and buried her head in her lap. Connie's aunt unclasped her stiff hands at last and began to stroke her hair.

Connie closed the door.

It really was most peculiar the way you could feel happy, yet so lonely at the same time.

33

For a while the newspapers were full of the story of Mr Thurston's death.

Death Fall in House of Heiress
Joyful Reunion Shadowed by Sorrow

Family Tragedy Blights Heiress's Happiness
Fatal Fall Flabbergasts Family

The verdict of the inquest was Accidental Death. Connie thought it had come to the right conclusion. If Leonard Crake hadn't turned up, though, what might have happened? It wasn't worth thinking about, so she didn't.

The funeral was poorly attended. It seemed that Harold Thurston hadn't had many friends.

But as the earth covered his coffin, Connie saw

Frank lurking among the yew trees. He didn't look particularly sorry either. Since Mr Thurston's death he had not returned to Alfred Place West to sleep, but only to pick up his clothes. She didn't think he knew the full truth about his father but she wasn't sure. What exactly had Frank been doing in Fulham that day? Had he been instructed by his father to threaten Mrs Crake, to stop her talking to Connie – or what?

As Connie, the aunts and Ida and Arthur were leaving for the waiting carriages, Frank sauntered across the gravel path. He looked as handsome as ever, even clad from head to foot in mourning black.

Connie noticed that Aunt Dorothea did her best not to recoil as he kissed her on the cheek. 'Your father, Frank,' she began. 'You must be grieving—'

'A sad day,' he interrupted, looking at them all gathered protectively around Aunt Dorothea. Arthur put his arm round Ida and glared. Frank stared at Connie, but then his eyes fell. 'A loss to us all.'

'Yes . . .' said Aunt Dorothea doubtfully. 'What shall you do, Frank, now he's gone?'

'I'm back off to the States,' he said cheerfully. 'Only place for me. London's a dull old hole. New York is where the new century has taken off!'

'Good luck,' she said faintly, but none of them could echo it.

The day after the funeral Connie was sitting with Ida and Arthur in the drawing-room. Music lessons had been forgotten during the exciting events of the past week, the piano in the corner abandoned. All Ida and Arthur wanted to do was to ask Connie questions, while they sat close together on the sofa and held hands.

Without Mr Thurston taking up half the room, it was much bigger. The whole house had seemed to breathe a sigh of relief at his demise and become spacious and light. The strangest thing was that the damp patches on the walls, the watchful heads, were fading and shrinking; Connie was sure they were, even the one in her bedroom.

Ida, of course, had not been there when Connie had accused Mr Thurston during her momentous speech at the garden party, so she had even more questions than Arthur.

'There were several things that helped me solve the mystery,' said Connie. 'I didn't always notice them at the time, but they must have stuck in my mind.

'Mr Crabb, the man at the Sisters of Hope, said that there was something about you, Ida, that made him want to protect you. Arthur felt the same. So did I.

'When Sadie Turner told me Leonard Crake had a key to the basement door here, I thought that if he really wanted to hurt you, he could have used it and come in at any time. I began to wonder if he wasn't out to harm you, after all. Then I saw him watching you at the garden party. He didn't look like a murderer. He looked like a *guardian*.

'That's why he was always following us at the beginning. He thought he could protect you from Mr Thurston, even though he sent you here as part of his plan.

'But you were frightened of him. You said it was because he would make you go back to the orphanage, but I didn't believe you, especially when Arthur and I discovered you'd left the orphanage a year ago! Then Ethel said something about knowing the "Captain" beforehand and then finding him at Madame Vichani's. I realised Mr Crake and the "Captain" were the same person and he'd been there with you, too.'

Ida put her hands to her face. 'I was a prisoner in Madame Vichani's house, play-acting in those blooming awful séances! The only way out seemed to be to agree to pretend to be Ida Fairbanks and I'd get a share of the money if I did. After I left I kept worrying that Crake was checking up on me, making sure I was going to get it.'

Arthur held her close as tears welled in her eyes.

'I hated deceiving you all! I used to cry about it when I was alone at night. I can't tell you how much I wanted a real mother. I couldn't confess the truth because I'd lose her. And then, of course, I fell in love with Arthur.' She looked at him shyly.

'Crake was a wicked man, sweetheart,' said Arthur, holding her tighter.

'Not wholly wicked,' said Connie. 'A bit of him was trying to be good.'

'Has he still got the key?' said Ida, a little nervously.

Connie smiled. 'No, Bessie found it on the kitchen table afterwards. I think it was his way of saying goodbye.'

She shook her head. 'Mrs Goodenough and Madame Vichani were worse, because they both had an income from their jobs. Leonard Crake was poor because he had left his life of crime behind and had no steady job. But the three of them couldn't resist getting their hands on Ida's fortune.'

'When did you suspect Mr Thurston, Connie?' said Arthur.

'Aunt Sylvie said things that made me realise that he was behind everything that had happened,' said Connie. 'I think she knew all along, but she couldn't trust her memory.

'Mr Thurston was the one who had the strongest motive for murder. Aunt Sylvie told me he thought the Fairbanks fortune would go to Aunt Dorothea if Ida was out of the way. He'd married my aunt when she was very frail because he hoped she'd die soon. He knew there was money in her family and hoped it would come to him.

'He thought little Ida would be presumed dead by the court. It must have been a double shock when he realised that Aunt Dorothea was made of stronger stuff than he expected and that the trustees had persuaded the court that Ida shouldn't be presumed dead at all until her eighteenth birthday and that the inheritance would be held in trust. So he had a long time to wait.

'I noticed the strange way Mr Thurston reacted when Aunt Dorothea told him that Ida had been found. He thought they'd discovered her corpse! When Ida appeared, he knew she must be an imposter but he had to keep quiet.

'And he encouraged the newspapers to write the story of her reappearance. He wanted to cover his tracks and see Ida accepted by society.

'He went a bit mad in the end. I don't think he would have taken the knife otherwise. What he needed desperately was a way out of his debts. Your death was the answer, Ida, because then your fortune would go to Aunt Dorothea and he knew he'd be able to get his hands on it, as he always had done with her money. It served his purpose to keep her under his thumb and make her believe she was an invalid.'

Ida gave a shudder. The three of them sat in silence for a moment. Then there was a tremendous grinding of brakes and the blast of a horn outside.

Connie rushed to the window.

A familiar figure with red hair that was fiery in the sunlight waved her driving goggles madly and gestured at the empty seats in her motor-car.

'It's Lavender!' exclaimed Connie. 'Who's coming for a drive?'

A week later Connie, Ida and the aunts were sitting at breakfast in Alfred Place. The sun was slanting in through the windows and shining on the walls, making the damp patches invisible in the light. The summer was warming at last after a wet, chilly beginning and middle.

Ida waved her engagement ring to and fro in the sunshine, so that it glittered in the beams. Arthur had spent all he could on it. It was small but shiny, and she was delighted with it. Aunt Dorothea said the wedding shouldn't take place for another year: Ida was still very young and Arthur must finish at the Royal College of Music.

Arthur had not yet appeared, but would do so shortly; Aunt Dorothea worried that he didn't get enough to eat in his lodgings, so he turned up for a late breakfast almost every day.

Sometimes Robert sloped in, too. He said their breakfasts were much more interesting than next door's.

The post had been. Bessie brought the letters in on a tray, as she always did. Though Mr Thurston's estate amounted to almost nothing, there had been other money matters to sort out – including those to do with the Fairbanks inheritance, now the courts had recognised Ida as the rightful beneficiary – so the letters were usually very dull indeed.

But today there was one in a thick cream envelope, addressed in large black handwriting to Aunt Sylvie.

She laid her hand on it and raised her eyes to the ceiling. There was a pause while everyone looked at her expectantly. At last she declared in triumph, 'Cousin Flossie!'

She tore the envelope open, leaving it stained with marmalade. 'There, I knew it was from her! The spirits are at work!'

'She's not dead, is she?' asked Connie.

'No, dear. What I meant was that sometimes unseen presences guide us. They have guided my cousin, who knows nothing of Harold's death, to write this letter!'

'She might have read about it in the newspapers,' said Connie.

'Not in Scotland! They have different papers there, I'm sure.'

Aunt Sylvie read the letter quickly. 'She's invited your aunt and me to her husband's estate to join a shooting party for the last two weeks of August.' She smiled delightedly at Aunt Dorothea. 'It's such a long time since we saw them, isn't it, dear? Why don't we go?'

Aunt Dorothea hesitated. 'I was going to put the house on the market . . .'

Aunt Sylvie waved her piece of toast dismissively. 'You can still do it. The agent can look after all that. You need a change.' Somehow, since Mr Thurston's death, Aunt Sylvie had become much more practical.

'Perhaps I do,' said Aunt Dorothea. She looked pleased and hopeful and all at once much younger.

There was an impatient knocking on the front door, which could only be Arthur. He always knocked to a little tune – da, da, dada da.

Ida jumped to her feet in joy and they heard her tripping along the hall.

Connie chewed her toast thoughtfully.

'Did you always know Ida was your daughter?' she asked Aunt Dorothea.

'I wanted so much to believe it that I think I truly did! But it wouldn't have mattered if she hadn't been. I love Ida for herself now.'

Arthur burst into the dining-room, accompanied by a smiling Ida. He, too, had a letter in his hand, this one typewritten on heavily embossed paper.

'Splendid news, Mrs T! Just listen to this! A rich American called Waldo Bamberger – he owns the Shining Seas shipping line – has asked me to play the piano to entertain the guests at dinner on a passage to New York in two weeks' time! It's the maiden voyage of a liner called the *Princess May*, his biggest yet. He apologises for the short notice, but his pianist has fallen ill. He happened to attend the garden party and heard me play. And Ida is invited too –' he kissed her '– as he's seen our engagement in the social columns! We'll travel first class, think of that! All expenses paid and a fee as well!'

'New York – think of that, Mother!' cried Ida.

'I'm not sure you should go,' said Aunt Dorothea. Her anxious expression hadn't quite vanished for ever because now it came back. 'You're only engaged, Ida, not married. It's not quite respectable.'

'Oh, please, Mother!' Ida hopped from foot to foot.

'Well . . .'

The sight of Ida's pleading face would persuade Aunt Dorothea in the end, Connie knew.

She looked at her plate. No one seemed to have noticed that she wasn't included in either of the invitations. The thought of being left in Alfred Place

West with only Bessie for company, while everyone else was away doing exciting things, was unbearable.

Aunt Sylvie spoke up unexpectedly. Perhaps she sensed the great wave of misery coming from Connie over the dining-room table.

'Why don't you let Connie go with Ida as chaperone? They can share a cabin.'

'Connie? A chaperone?' said Aunt Dorothea doubtfully. 'She's a little young.'

'But wise for her years,' said Aunt Sylvie.

'Oh, yes, Connie must come with us!' cried Ida. 'I'll pay for her ticket. I've got heaps of money now! We need her to look after us, don't we, Arthur?'

'Oh, absolutely! We can't manage without Connie,' agreed Arthur.

The sadness in Connie's heart eased as Aunt Dorothea looked around them all and smiled. 'I suppose so.'

It was settled.

New York! The most thrilling city in the world and she, Constance Clementine Carew, would be going there!

Connie could hardly believe it. She thought dreamily of the Statue of Liberty, the skyscrapers of Manhattan, Broadway, the Brooklyn Bridge. What opportunities the trip would offer a budding anthropologist! A whole new people to study – the Americans!

A thought struck her aunt.

'But you will bring Ida back, won't you, Arthur? Don't be tempted to stay there by your Mr Bamberger. I couldn't bear to lose her again. She belongs with us, at least until your wedding.'

'Of course, Mrs T,' said Arthur cheerfully.

'Do I belong too?' asked Connie, in a small voice.

It slipped out without her meaning to say it. But it was suddenly a very important question. Perhaps it had been all along.

Aunt Dorothea glanced at Connie and saw her face. Unexpectedly, she rose to her feet and put her arms tight around her.

'Of course you belong, my darling Connie,' she said. 'You always have. That goes without saying.'

Still, Connie was glad Aunt Dorothea *had* said it.

For now, that was all she wanted to know.